CRY FOR ME

ERIN TREJO

CRY FOR ME

ERIN TREJO

1
———

KNOX

The sound of the tattoo gun buzzing as the ink and needle sinks into my flesh calms me slightly. I've been on edge lately with good reason. Everything seems to be happening in one shitstorm after another. A vicious never-ending cycle that none of us can control. First my dad and then our mom. I shake my head and glance down at the cross my friend, Danny, is inking into my flesh. A reminder of who I am and what I've done that can never be forgiven. This is my way of settling the demons in my head. Letting them know they can't rule me forever no matter how easy it would be to let them. One day I'll find my way just like my brothers have. Today isn't that day.

"You want any color in this?" Danny asks when he glances up at me.

"No. Leave that shit as black as my soul," I tell him. He chuckles and gets back to work. I close my eyes and let the sound drag me to another place. A place that doesn't include all the hell we've lived the past year. I've always known that family means everything, but at the same time, it was my supposed family that ripped us all apart. From my dad being the vicious bastard that he was, to my mom trying to ruin my brother's whole world just for money, I've seen firsthand how family can fuck you faster than an enemy. I've also learned from it. I don't think I can let anyone near my heart, not the way Callan and Steele have. I feel like a piece of me has been crushed and ruined for anyone to come. Maybe I'm jaded or maybe I just don't want the complications that come along with love.

"You're done," Danny says, setting his gun on the counter before cleaning me up. I shove out of the chair and move in front of the mirror to take a look. A large cross with jagged edges and a black rose in the middle adorn the left side of my chest now. It's perfect.

"Looks good, man. I appreciate you getting me in," I say when I turn to face him.

"Always, Knox. You're one of my best customers and you let me go crazy." He smirks at me. It's true. Since I've been coming to Danny, I've given him free rein of my flesh. Whatever he thinks would look good, I let him run with it. His creativity is something I've never seen before.

"You kick ass, too. You shouldn't be sitting around here in this tiny ass shop, man."

"You tell me that every time you're in here."

"It's true." Grabbing my shirt, I toss it over my shoulder and head for the door with Danny behind me. We walk down the hall when someone comes barreling toward us and slams into me. A firm body presses against me and I almost snap. Grabbing the girl by the wrist, I shove her back a step.

"In a hurry?" I snarl.

"Maybe." Big brown eyes stare back at me as I shove her back another step.

"Shit. Sorry, Liz. I forgot we had a session. Go on in there and I'll be in, in a minute," Danny says, stepping around us and walking toward the front. I don't let her wrist go as I stare down at her.

"You might want to watch who you run into. Not all men are as nice he is." I growl low in my throat as I nod after Danny.

"He only does it because we're related."

"Lucky him." Shoving her back a step, she stumbles before righting herself. Her hands clench at her sides, her nostrils flaring as she steps closer to me.

"I don't know who didn't suck your cock this morning but don't take your bullshit out on me," she says through gritted teeth. Her eyes stay on mine, a silent challenge that I'd like to play with but I won't. Instead, I chuckle and walk past her, shoulder checking her on my way past.

"Prick," I hear her say as I chuckle and step out into the front lobby. Danny's at the desk with another one of his employees when I move to stand in front of the desk.

"You need another appointment?" he asks with a smirk.

"Not yet. You coming down to the reopening of Intensity Friday night?" Danny isn't much into the dance scene but it helps his business. The more we can show off his work, the more people show up to his shop, and I'm all about helping my friends.

"I don't know. Liz is in town and shit," he says, scrubbing his hand over his face.

"Who is she anyway?"

"My cousin. We used to be pretty close, then she moved out to New York with her boyfriend and we haven't talked much. I'm not even sure what she's doing here to be honest. When Liz shows up, she usually drags trouble along with her." I nod my head as if I understand. Hell, I do to a point. Trouble seems to always surround the Alder men, anymore.

"Bring her with. Let's have a good time. I'm sure the guys would love to see you."

"Yeah, I'll think about it."

"Good. I'll let you get back to work. Thanks for hooking me up, man." Danny walks around the desk and pulls me into a hug before he turns and heads back into the back of the shop. I turn on my heel and step out into the cool night air and inhale deeply. With everything going on lately, I've been feeling a little lost in my head. No, not just in my head, but in general. I need something to get my head together. Maybe the reopening of Intensity will do just that.

2

LIZ

They won't find me here. They wouldn't even think to search here. That's what I'm telling myself as I stroll the halls of Alder Academy with my book bag over my shoulder, holding the strap tightly in my hand. Security is insane at this place. I'm safe. At least I hope I am.

I let my eyes travel over the other students that walk the halls on their way to class, noting how normal they all seem. High class? Yes, but normal to some degree. I don't really fit into that category, but then again, who really cares right? I'm not here to fit in but I also don't want to stick out. That's when I see a girl leaning against the door with a cigarette between her lips. I watch her blow smoke through her nose appearing as though she could give two fucks if anyone sees her or not. That's who I need to befriend.

Strolling in that direction, I step outside and glance toward her. She notices and raises her eyebrow at me.

"Can I help you with something?" Okay, maybe she isn't the

right person to become friends with. I start to turn and head back in when she stops me.

"I'm Whisper."

"Liz. Do you have another?" Her face lights up when I nod at her cigarette. She pulls her pack out and offers it to me. Taking one out, I light it up and stand next to her.

"Smoking isn't allowed on campus," a deep voice sounds from next to us. I don't turn to look as panic creeps in. Just what I don't need, to get in trouble the first day here.

"As if I give a fuck. What do you want, Callan?" Whisper glances over as I peer up. A tall muscular dark-haired beauty stands next to her, a smirk on his perfect face.

"For a dancer, you sure smoke a lot."

"Only when I'm stressed," she adds.

"Why are you stressed? What did my brother do now?" His hand comes up to swipe a piece of hair away from her face.

"Nothing. I'm just nervous about Intensity."

"Everything is fine. We have extra security all around and even here at school. Besides, she's gone," the man adds. I flick my cigarette to the ground and snuff it out with my shoe before I start to turn and head back inside.

"Thanks for the smoke," I say softly when a hand catches my wrist. I lower my gaze and follow the hand back up to the man that was just talking to Whisper.

"Callan, don't manhandle her," Whisper hisses and swats at his arm. He releases me but not before letting his gaze roam my body.

"You're new."

"Clearly," Whisper snorts.

"Who are you? I didn't know we were getting anyone new," he adds, his eyes dancing with mischief.

"I'm Liz."

"Liz? Just Liz?" he asks.

"Yeah, just Liz. Like Cher or Sting. Can I go?" I ask, becoming agitated with him already. I don't need to stand here and tell him my life story. Whisper laughs and moves past him, wrapping her arm around mine.

"I like her already! Bye, Callan!" She drags me through the door before she asks, "What class do you have?"

"Dance." Her eyes jerk to mine and a smile tugs across her face.

"This is awesome. We have that class together. That was Callan, by the way. They own the school."

"Wait, what? He owns it?" I ask confused. Whisper doesn't appear shocked at all as she leads me down the hall.

"Him and his brothers, Steele and Knox. They're good guys. Moody as hell but you get used to it."

"You're friends with them?" I ask as we make our way down the hall. It seems Whisper is a lot like me in the outcast depart-ment. She isn't all dressed up in heels and makeup like most of the girls here. She's in yoga pants and a long shirt with a pair of combat boots.

"You could say that. I'm with Steele. Well, I don't honestly know what you would call it. Dating seems stupid since we live together," she adds holding the door and ushering me inside. It takes seconds for Whisper to be lifted off the floor and tossed over someone's shoulder. She squeals before slapping at his back. Once on the other side of the room, he drops her to her feet and presses her against the glass mirror. I notice the teacher roll her eyes and that alone makes me grin. I think I like Whisper a little more now. I start heading that direction when someone rushes past, shoulder checking me on the way. I stumble forward but right myself quickly.

"Knox! You fucking asshole. Watch out!" Whisper screams

as she comes toward me. "You okay?" Before I can answer, she's spinning around and storming toward the man she called Knox. She has his shirt fisted in her hand as she snarls at him.

"I'm fine," I add, hoping to calm the tension between the two.

"I don't know what your problem is today, but stop being a dick to my friends or I'll cut your fucking nuts off," she snaps before his eyes come to meet mine. That's him. The same asshole from Danny's shop. Just great. A sick smirk crosses those plump lips as he gets closer. He reaches out, tugging on a strand of my hair.

"You're picking up strays now, Whisper?" As quickly as his hand was there, she slaps it away.

"She isn't a stray, you asshole. I like her."

"You would," he huffs.

"What the hell is that supposed to mean?" I ask, crossing my arms over my chest. Knox's eyes fall to my low-cut shirt right before I drop my arms. He chuckles when the other guy steps up next to him.

"Stop messing with Whisper's toys," Callan says. He's the same one from outside.

"Looks like an interesting toy."

"Knox, I mean it. Leave her alone." Whisper shoves him back a step but he just laughs and walks away. "You'll get used to these assholes."

"I'm not an asshole and frankly, I'm a little upset that you'd call me that. I'm hurt, Whisper," Callan says, placing his hand over his heart.

"Keep on, Callan, and I'm telling Shane. She will have your balls in a grinder." Callan laughs before moving back, standing next to his brother. Whisper loops her arm with mine once more and leads me off to the side as the teacher starts talking.

"She's annoying," I say under my breath.

"She is, but she's also our way to passing the damn class. Do you dance?"

"A little. I used to hang out in nightclubs a lot." Whisper nods and looks toward the teacher as I do the same. That's when the music starts and so does my heart.

3

KNOX

I drop to the floor and roll my hips. If you didn't know me, you would think I was part of the *Magic Mike* strip show. I buck my hips before spinning around and peering up at the new teacher. Miss Johnson is older but still knows what she's doing. She isn't impressed with my dance moves, but she doesn't try to stop me either. Maybe it's because she likes the free show. I can see most of the girls in here do too. Maybe that's why I do it.

"Get it, Knox!" Whisper calls out. I smirk and leap to my feet, grabbing her friend by the wrist and dragging her into the middle of the room. I grind against her but she remains still. Her eyes track my movements, but she doesn't make any kind of attempt to move with me. Maybe she can't dance. Maybe she's a prude. Either way, I keep moving. I grab her around the waist and before she can say anything, I have her on her back on the floor. I part her thighs as I roll my hips watching her eyes the whole time. The room is going insane, which they always do when one of us Alder boys gets in a mood. Today just happens to be my day.

"Are you going to move with me?" I ask as my breaths come in pants.

"Not a chance in hell." I smirk at her response.

"Suit yourself." I grab her and jump up, pulling her with me when she shocks me. She starts to move and just like that, she has me around the neck, grinding herself against me. My hand comes to her hip, trying to halt her movements but she spins out and presses her ass right against my cock. There isn't anything I can do to stop it from rising. My fingers dig into her flesh when she finally stops moving. I lean down and brush my lips against her ear.

"Is that all you've got?"

She huffs a laugh. "Hell no. You just won't be getting any of my good moves." With that, she walks back toward Whisper, leaving me standing on my own trying to catch my breath. Miss Johnson goes on talking when Callan strolls toward me.

"That was an interesting start to the day," he says with a chuckle.

"It was wasn't it?"

"She going to be a problem for you?" he asks. I glance over at her and shake my head.

"Hell no. She might just become my new favorite toy."

"Are you kidding me?" Callan glares at me like I committed a crime. I just shake my head.

"What's wrong? You get your girl and suddenly I can't play games?" Narrowing my eyes, I study my brothers face waiting for him to say something wrong. Something that will have me snapping his neck in front of the whole class.

"Go for it, man. I think Whisper likes her though," he adds

nodding over his shoulder. I follow the direction and find Whisper happily talking to the girl. That doesn't mean shit.

"Too bad for her," I mumble. Callan laughs, slapping a hand on my shoulder before turning and walking away. I move toward my bag and grab my towel, wiping the sweat from my face when she speaks.

"That's all the moves you have? Are you a stripper?" I turn slowly and my eyes collide with her dark brown ones.

"I'm not a stripper."

"Then what's with the stripper moves in class? Did you think you were impressing someone?" She raises an eyebrow, challenging me. It's cute. I take a step closer to her and watch her for a reaction that I never get. Hmm, she isn't scared. That makes it all the more fun.

"I don't need to impress anyone. I usually get what I want in the end, anyway."

"That's the line you're using? Pathetic," she huffs. She turns and starts to walk away when I snap. Grabbing her around the waist, I lift her before slamming her against the wall. The air escapes her lungs in a puff as Miss Johnson hollers at me to stop.

"I don't need lines. I don't need a strip show. I don't need anything but these two hands to get what I want, Liz." I can see her breath fog the mirror as she breathes in and out. My body is pressed right into the back of hers and fuck does she feel good beneath me.

"Well, if you don't get those two hands off me, I might just decide to cut them the fuck off. Then how will you get what you want?" She's being serious. She isn't afraid like most girls. Whisper steps toward us but I see Callan pull her back. He whispers in her ear and she nods her head reluctantly.

"You're new here, so I'll let that slide this time. Stay out of my way or you won't like the way I play," I warn her. She isn't really in my way so much as she's now on my radar. Something about this girl is nagging at me. I need to ask Danny about her, but he already said she always comes with trouble. I just so happen to like trouble.

"The last guy that threatened me, nearly lost his cock," she says, and it sounds like a warning. I chuckle darkly near her ear before biting the lobe hard enough to draw blood. She gasps as our eyes connect in the mirror.

"I'll take that challenge and raise you one. The last girl that got in my way killed herself. Let that sink in." Pulling away from her, I grab my bag and toss it over my shoulder as I head for the door. No one says a word, they're all used to us coming and going as we please. Either way, we're going to pass the class with no issues.

I storm through the hall and out the front door when my phone rings. I slide it out and answer, knowing it's Steele.

"What?"

"Why are you causing trouble?"

"I'm not. Just having a little fun is all." When I get to my truck, I lean against it and wait to see what else he has to say.

"Not what I heard, but as long as it's all fun and games, go for it."

"Wasn't aware I needed your permission," I add.

"You don't. Hey, I was calling to see if you could stop by Intensity and see if Leddy needs anything else before Friday. She isn't answering the phone," he says.

"Yeah, fine. I'm heading that way now."

"You sure you're okay?"

"No. I was honestly thinking about hitting the cabin for a few days. Taking a break and recharging," I finally admit. I hear Steele sigh into the phone.

"If that's what you need, do it, Brother. I want your head at a hundred percent. I know the last couple of months have been something out of a goddamn movie, and I don't blame you for needing a break. As long as it isn't a permanent one." I smirk at his words.

"If I didn't know any better, I'd think you actually cared about me, Steele."

"Fuck you. It's always been the three of us, Knox. Nothing and no one changes that," he reminds me.

"I know. I'll talk to you when I get home. We ordering in?"

"Yeah. We'll get something." The line goes dead as I climb in the truck and toss my bag over the seat. I'm about to rev up the engine when I see her. Her hands are flying through the air as Danny stands in front of her. I wonder what the hell that's about. She looks pissed but he looks downright murderous. I want to go over there and ask what's going on, but that's not my concern. Instead, I shift the truck into drive and head toward Intensity.

4

———

LIZ

"I don't see how that's my problem," I say with a shrug of my shoulders.

"Are you serious right now, Liz?" Danny roars. What does he want from me? I'm doing the best I can.

"Yes, I'm dead serious. See what I did there?" I smirk and give him a wink. He doesn't appear impressed.

"This is serious and death jokes aren't helping, Liz." I roll my eyes and heft my bag up my shoulder as I look at him.

"I know it is, but I'm fine. In fact, I'm better than fine. They won't search here. They don't even know about you, and if it's that big of a problem just stay away from me, Danny." Not that it's what I want, but at the same time I don't want to risk Danny being in the middle of another of my messes. It's not like he hasn't seen that train wreck before. He runs his hand through his hair as he glances around the parking lot.

"This is probably the safest school there is. Their security is intense."

"So are the students," I say.

"Some of them. Look, if you feel off or you notice anything, just promise me you'll tell me," he basically pleads with me. I nod my head and wrap my arms around his waist hugging him.

"I promise, I will tell you."

"Good. Now don't forget that we're having dinner on Saturday and if you want to hit that club Friday let me know." I pull away and nod my head as he smiles at me. "Behave!" he adds, pointing at me.

"When do I not behave?" He laughs a hearty laugh before walking away.

"I like you." I turn to see Whisper standing behind me.

"I might like you too. What's up?"

"Not much. Getting the hell out of here. You want to hang out?" I debate saying no because frankly, I don't know her, but what's it really going to hurt?

"Sure."

"Good. I'm ready for a drink," she says, making me laugh as we walk through the parking lot.

"It's only three in the afternoon."

"I'm a day drinker. So fucking what?" She laughs, causing me to laugh along with her. Whisper walks to a truck and opens the door, motioning for me to climb in the other side. I do and sink into the leather seat as she starts it up.

"Big truck for a small girl," I tease.

"Yeah, Steele didn't need it today, so I took it. He's probably at home frothing at the mouth as we speak." She rolls her eyes.

"What's he like?"

"Intense. You'll see. Where do you think we're going to day drink?" She laughs as she pulls out onto the main road. I swallow hard, hoping like hell I didn't make the wrong choice here. I don't know her. I don't know them. From what I've been hearing, they run this city and that's not something I really need to be in the middle of. It makes me a target, and if they make a huge deal of me being here, my name could pop up for others. That's not a risk I'm willing to take, but it's a little late for that now.

We pull up in front of a massive house that has me doing a double take. Whisper kills the engine and hops out of the truck as I do the same.

"You live here?"

"Long story short? This used to be their dad's house. He's dead. We moved in. It's huge, yes, but the guys have their own space which with the three of them is needed."

"Are they that bad?" I ask, not sure I want the answer to that.

"No, but they are all alpha pricks, which means there is a shit ton of testosterone in here." Whisper shoves the door open and walks in as I follow behind her. She doesn't stop until we walk into what appears to be a living room. She grabs bottles out of a small fridge and turns to me with a smile. That smile quickly fades and I'm confused until I feel hands slip around my waist. I'm about to fight when they tighten.

"Who is this?" a man asks close to my ear.

"First of all, get your hands off her, Steele."

"And second?"

"She's my friend and you aren't allowed to touch her," Whisper says, popping the top on one of the bottles and taking a long pull.

"Day drinking again, I see."

"Still touching my friend, I see," she retorts. I try to pull away from him but he's too strong. Whisper rolls her eyes as if this is a natural occurrence around here. I roll my head forward ready to crack him in the face if he doesn't let go when Whisper laughs. The guy releases me, shoving me a little when I slam into someone else.

"Thought I told you to stay out of my way." When I lift my gaze, I see it's Knox that's in front of me.

"What just happened here?" Steele asks, observing all of us.

"She was about to head butt you!" Whisper laughs hysterically. Steele looks to me while Knox grabs a hold of my wrist and jerks me closer.

"No, she wasn't," Steele says before walking toward Whisper.

"Why are you here?" Knox asks, leaning into my space.

"Whisper invited me."

"Why are you here is a better question? I asked you to run by Intensity," Steele chimes in. I watch as he takes the bottle from Whisper and brings it to his lips.

"I made a pit stop. Now I can take our new friend on a field trip," Knox says slowly, running his fingers up my arm.

"She doesn't want you, Knox," Whisper points out.

"Sure she does," he retorts.

"No, I'm pretty sure I don't."

"Too bad that isn't your decision to make. Whisper didn't want me at first either, did you Whisper?" A gasp catches in my throat as I look between the three of them. Whisper just smirks, Steele isn't paying much attention, and Knox is smiling like a goddamn fool.

What the hell did I just get myself into?

5

KNOX

"Let me out of this truck," she says, sounding a bit panicked. It's cute.

"No."

"You can't just kidnap me," she snaps, crossing her arms over her chest and glaring at me.

"I think I just did," I tease. That's when she does it. She reaches for the door handle and throws the door open while I'm doing seventy. In the blink of an eye, she is pulling at her seatbelt. She's going to jump! Holy shit, the girl has a set of balls on her. I swerve the truck, grabbing her wrist as I do so she can't fall out. Slamming on the brakes, she whips forward, her head hitting the dashboard.

"What the fuck is wrong with you?" I roar as I unbuckle myself. I release her and hop out of the truck coming around to her side and pull her out. Slamming her against the side of the truck, I see the speck of blood on her head.

"You wouldn't let me out!"

"I was driving, you little psycho!"

"I didn't ask to go with you, did I?" she snaps as she reaches up to rub her head.

"You're probably the dumbest girl I've ever met in my life."

"Coming from you, I'm sure that's a compliment." Damn it, she's hell on earth. I like it.

"You show up in my town, my school, and then my house and you think you have a say in anything?" I raise an eyebrow and move in closer. Her body is pressed into the side of the truck, trapped by me. She peers up and there's a slight dizziness in her gaze. Shit, how hard did she hit her head? Reaching up, I run my fingers near the cut watching the way her breath catches.

"I didn't know it was your town," she sasses back.

"Now you do."

"So what? I should run and cower? Find a new school?"

"For starters. Unless you don't mind the games I like to play," I remind her.

"Which are?" She'd like to know. Yeah, right.

"Which you only get to see when I decide to play them." I lean down so that my lips are close to hers but she doesn't move. In fact, she doesn't even breathe when I'm this close to her.

"You can't scare me."

"Oh, I bet I can." I smirk. "Like right now. You're not sure if I'm going to kiss you or not. You're afraid that if I do, I won't stop there," I tell her. She smirks at me.

"You have no idea who I am," she says softly, shaking her head from side to side. "If you were smart, you'd stay away from me. Far away because when shit goes south, I'm the last person you want to be near." I step back laughing, darkly. She clearly has no idea who the hell the Alder's are.

"We are the shit that goes south," I say, throwing my arms out to the sides. "We are the things that go bump in the night. If anyone should stay away, it's you, sweetheart." I watch her, the way her eyes stay locked with mine, the anger, the fear. There is something more to this girl than I originally thought. She's not lying. I can typically spot a liar from a mile away and this one? No, she's not lying. She truly believes that whatever it is that follows her is worse than we are.

"You don't scare me," she says, keeping her head high.

"Maybe I'm not trying to scare you. Yet." She steps away from the truck, unsteady on her feet. I watch her grab her bag and toss it over her shoulder before turning and walking away from me. I let her go this time. Next time, it won't be that easy to walk away from me. Next time, I'll show her exactly the kinds of games we like to play around here.

When she's far enough away, I hop back into the truck and put it in drive, heading for the club. Not like I feel like dealing with Leddy today either, but Steele asked me to.

It doesn't take me long to get there and head inside. The construction looks great. As soon as we could, we started to rebuild. Leddy wasn't happy that we threw money her way considering this was her place and not ours, but what she didn't understand was that this place means a lot to us too. It isn't just hers, not anymore. We all come here to let off some steam and whether she likes it or not, it's a part of us.

"What are you doing here?" Speak of the devil. I turn with a smile plastered to my face.

"What a way to say hello."

"You're an asshole. That's the only way to say it."

"Are we still fighting?" I ask, raising an eyebrow in her direction.

"You tell me. You're the one that's been treating me like garbage for a month now," she reminds me.

"You asked me to do the unthinkable, Leddy! How did you expect me to react?" I cock my head to the side and study her. I understand why she asked me but at the same time, it pissed me off.

"I didn't think they were that serious, Knox. What was I supposed to do? The two of you make my head spin!" She throws her hands in the air as I move closer. Reaching up, I wrap my hand around the back of her neck and pull her closer to me.

"Asking me to help you break up my brother and his girl should have never crossed your mind, Leddy. He's off-limits," I say grinding my teeth.

"I know that now, and I said I was sorry, Knox. What more do you want from me?" I lean down, brushing my lips over her cheek, listening as she sucks in a breath.

"I don't want anything from you. I want you to stay away from them," I remind her.

"I have been. I'm trying here, Knox. We've all been friends for a long time and I don't want to lose that." When I pull back, I see the pink coloring her cheeks, and I wonder what it would be like to fuck her one good time against the wall of this club. It's not like I haven't thought about it.

"Then don't make us walk, Leddy." She nods her head and I release my hold on her as she steps back. "Steele said you haven't been answering your phone."

"With good reason. I'm busy."

"Do you need anything for Friday? You all set?" I ask, walking around as the finishing touches are being put into place. The place looks the same, yet different.

"Everything is set but there is something I want to talk to you about," she says. I turn to face her and wait. "The competition. The one in Florida is in a few months."

"You're going?" I ask. She nods.

"If I can get a partner." There it is.

"No."

"Come on, Knox. It would be good money for the club and all that attention? The media will go insane," she nearly begs. I run my hand through my hair as I think about it. I know that this means a lot to her, and I also know that before Whisper, Steele had planned on doing it with her, but now that isn't really an option.

"Fine. I'll do it."

"You will?" Her eyes light up as she leaps into my arms. I wrap my arms around her and hold her, feeling her body pressed against mine. There's been this weird tension between Leddy and me for a while now. We've both felt it and when she told me how she felt about me and Steele, I almost acted on it. I thought better of it considering how long we've been friends, and I can't really see myself long term with her but touching her right now? Fuck, that feels good.

"Strictly business," I tell her just as my lips come to rest on her neck. She gasps and tightens her body around me. I groan as I walk us toward the wall, pressing her body against it.

"What are you doing?" she whispers softly.

"Fucking things up. Making them worse? I don't really know." My lips trail down her neck, and I feel her body shudder in my arms. I suck her flesh into my mouth knowing this is a bad idea.

"What the hell is this?" I pull back and let out a sigh of relief when I hear Callan's voice. I let Leddy's body slowly slide down mine until her feet hit the floor.

"This is me getting the fuck out of here," I tell him as I spin and head for the door. He follows. Of course, he follows.

"You and Leddy?" he says as I make my way to the truck.

"No."

"Really, Knox?" I turn to face my little brother as he stands there with his arms crossed over his chest.

"Not what you think it is, Brother."

"You weren't just about to fuck her against the wall of the club?" he asks in amusement.

"Maybe." I smirk.

"So, what is it? You two together now?" I run my hand over my face and shake my head.

"No. It was… fuck. It just happened. It won't happen again." Callan nods his head as I shake my head. Since everything went down with our dad and our mom, things in my head have been off. I can't shake the bad feelings that slip through my veins.

"It's almost Thanksgiving," Callan states.

"And?"

"And we're family, Knox. We are going to have a good holiday," he tells me. I don't know how true that is. I can't seem to get myself under control.

"Yeah. We'll see."

6

LIZ

I yawn and roll over to view the clock. Two in the freaking morning. Why am I awake? I close my eyes and beg sleep to come back to me, but when I hear the noise that woke me the first time, I freak out. My heart leaps into my throat as I climb out of the bed. Rolling Springs is too nice of a city to have a bad side of town but I'm in it. Crawling across the floor, I climb to my knees and peek out the window. The alley is dark outside my apartment, only the slight light of the moon shining. I can see a shadow but I can't make out much more. Dropping back to my hands and knees, I crawl to the bedside table and grab my phone, calling Danny. Glass shatters as my heart leaps into my throat. I can't call the police. No, they would know. They could track me.

"Pick up. Pick up," I chant softly as my heart bangs against my ribcage. More noises sound outside my window and I scoot across the floor to the closet. Once I'm tucked inside, I bring the phone back to my ear.

"What's wrong?"

"Someone's in the alley, Danny. I heard glass and—" Just as I'm about to say more, glass shatters from somewhere out front. I suck in a breath and pray they didn't find me.

"I'm on the way. Two minutes, Liz." I know the shop is just down the road. That's why I got this apartment, I knew it would be close to him. I can hear him on the other end of the line cursing and moving around. The sound of a car engine and doors slamming resonates through the phone. I keep my eyes tightly closed taking breaths so that I don't pass out. That's all I need. Then I hear it. Danny's screams from out front followed by the sounds of someone hitting the door. I leap to my feet, dropping my phone as I go. Running through the apartment, I unlock the door and pull it open to find Danny.

"Who was it? Was it them?"

"Who is them?" a slurred voice comes from behind Danny. Danny rolls his eyes and steps to the side to reveal Knox. A drunk Knox.

"What is this?" I ask, motioning between the two of them. Danny reaches up to wipe the blood away from his lip before reaching for Knox and dragging his half passed out body through the door. I step aside and take in what's happening.

"This drunken idiot was breaking shit in the alley. He broke your window too," Danny says, helping Knox onto the couch.

"What the hell is he doing in the alley?"

"*He's* right here you know?" Knox growls. I ignore his drunk ass.

"I don't know."

"I'm drunk that's what," he chimes in again.

"Clearly. Why were you outside my apartment?" I question him. His face wrinkles up as he glances around the room.

"You live in this shit?" Now it's my turn to roll my eyes.

"Take him home," I tell Danny.

"I can't. I have a client at the shop. I had to stop when you called." Shit and double shit.

"I'm sorry. Shit, Danny. Just… leave his ass on the couch then." Danny peers up at me giving me the 'are you sure' look. I fucked up his appointment, I can't force him to take Knox home now.

"Yeah. Come back in the morning though," I say pointing at Knox.

"I will. Love you, Liz."

"Love you too," I tell him as I watch him head out the front door. I move behind him and lock up before gazing at my window.

"Aww, you love him," Knox slurs.

"Shut the hell up." The weather is a little cooler now, winter is on its way. I don't have anything to board the window up with so I grab an extra blanket from the hall closet and hang it up there instead. If any idiot tries to come in, I would hope Knox would hear it. When I turn back, he's passed out on the couch. I decide to head back into my room, close the door and lock it behind me. Finding my phone, I set it back in its spot on the table and climb into bed. Fear is real for me. The things I've seen in the past, things I've had to endure. I can't let my guard down even if I wanted to.

Closing my eyes, I finally fall asleep. That doesn't stop the dreams from coming. I can see it all just like I did that night. I could hear the shots, see her fall. I could taste the metallic blood on my tongue and feel those arms wrap around me. I fought, trying to get free when I jolt awake. The sun is barely peeking through the curtains when I notice why I feel trapped.

"Get the hell off me!" I scream, shoving at Knox. He's not even awake. He pulls me harder against his body and sighs into the back of my hair.

"It's cold out there," he mumbles.

"You can't sleep here," I tell him, trying to remain calm when all I want to know is how he got in here without me hearing him. I should have heard him.

"It's warm. Just sleep," he grumbles. I move to lift his arm once more but he doesn't budge. With a huff, I adjust my position and close my eyes praying for at least another hour of sleep. Then I can deal with this. Deal with him.

Sleep must have taken over because I feel completely refreshed when I wake up. Knox isn't in the bed anymore and I'm thankful for that. I throw my legs over the side and stand, stretching as I go. I drag myself out into the kitchen to find a note saying someone would be by to fix the window. No, I'm sorry for breaking it or scaring the shit out of you. No, thank you for letting me sleep off my drunken bullshit. Not that it surprises me at all. Just as I'm about to make some instant coffee, someone knocks. I walk over and peek through the small peephole to see Danny. Unlocking the door, I pull it open as he holds up a bag of donuts.

"Why are you even alive at this hour?" I ask.

"I run on very little sleep. You okay?" I step aside and let him in as I nod.

"I'm fine. I'm really sorry about that."

"I want you to come stay with me."

"Not a chance in hell," I say as I grab my coffee mug.

"I mean it. My place has better protection."

"Don't knock my apartment," I laugh.

"I'm not. I'm just worried is all." I sit at the table next to him and grab his hand in my free one.

"I know and I'm sorry. I was freaked out a little and then Knox being in the alley…"

"Where is he anyway?"

"Left before I got up. He left a note saying he would have the window fixed," I add. Danny chuckles.

"Yeah, I'm sure he will. What are you doing today? Want me to finish up your ink?" My eyes light up and so does my heart.

"Yes!"

"Okay," he laughs. "Let's eat and then we can head over. Have you decided about the club tonight?" I reach into the bag and pull out a donut, taking a huge bite.

"Do you want to go?" I ask him.

"If you want to. I think it'll be fun. It's the reopening and they're having some competition dances too. You might like it," he says.

"Okay. Might as well, I don't have anything better to do."

"Good. You have to dress up," he says, raising an eyebrow.

"What are you trying to say? That I don't know how to dress?"

"Nope. Just saying that your normal baggy clothes won't cut it at that place."

"Really?" I've never really been to a club that made you dress up. We all kind of hung out in what we were wearing and that's it.

"Yeah. Intensity is all about its name. The people, the music, the clothes. You're going to love it," Danny tells me, grabbing a donut out and taking a bite. I guess I need to up my game tonight.

7

KNOX

W e're in the middle of the dance floor, me and Leddy, when Next's *Too Close* comes over the speakers. One of my all-time favorites. Leddy starts to march around the floor as my eyes follow her body, then she drops down, rolling her hips and popping back up. I smirk as she sways her hips and comes toward me. This isn't our usual dance music but she is making a point tonight. Her hand wraps around my neck as she rolls her body against mine. I start to move, pulling her closer as the crowd screams. I nod my head once and she pulls away. I spin her around, grab her hips and grind against her. Shoving her forward, she bends and arches her back. This dance is sexual as fuck and that's what I like about it. It's not just a dance, it's a mood. It's a feeling, one that can't be explained.

We keep moving when I see her. Liz. She's standing by Danny, her eyes wide as she watches us. Gripping Leddy's waist, I lift her. She wraps her legs around my waist as I buck my hips. She leans back, her hands planted on the floor before I shove her off me, watching her as she flips and comes down in a split before slowly wiggling her way back up. The crowd is going insane just like we knew they would. Two more dancers come into the middle just as I lick my lips and head toward Liz. I'm watching her like she's my prey and for tonight? She is. Danny laughs when I grab her hand and pull her toward me. She shakes her head and tries to pull away but I don't let her. Callan walks up behind her, grabbing her hips. She nearly jumps straight off the floor as we laugh.

"Calm down, it's only a dance," Callan says over the music. Liz glances over her shoulder at him before nodding slowly. Callan begins to move his hips, pressing against her. At first I'm not sure she's going to move an inch, but when I grab her hands and throw them over my shoulders, she slowly starts to roll her body. I nod my head letting her know to keep going. Her body begins to rock to the beat as I really get into it. Callan steps back once he sees she's starting to move with me. I run my hands down her sides, keeping her at pace with me. She's soft under my palms and my cock responds. Her eyes burn into mine as we move around the floor. She loosens up, follows my lead and before I know it, we're grinding like we're about to fuck right here and now. When I see the need in her eyes, I know it's time. I step back and spin around, grabbing some random girl and pulling her against me. I spin us enough to see Liz, the pink on her cheeks, the fire in her eyes. She's pissed that I left her standing there the way I did. I think she's going to run when she grabs Callan and jerks him into her arms. He laughs, throwing his head back and grabs her hips. Steele moves in behind her, and the three of them grind together when Whisper joins them. She shoves Callan out of her way and moves up close to Liz. I watch her for a reaction but I don't get one. Instead, she pulls Whisper in close, whispering something in her ear. Then before anyone can think, their lips collide. Steele stops moving, his jaw dropping. I shove the girl that I was dancing with off me and turn to walk away when Callan stops me.

"The player is being played." He laughs hysterically. I shrug him off and head toward the exit. Storming out, I'm pissed and don't even know why. As soon as I make it outside, I see her rush past me and around the corner of the club. Out of curiosity or maybe I'm just being a fucking prick, I follow her around. Liz is bent over, her hands on her knees as sobs shake her body.

"Not really the reaction I thought you'd have." Her head snaps up, her tear-filled eyes meeting mine.

"What did you think?" she asks, cocking her head to the side.

"Honestly? I thought you were about to fuck one of them on the dance floor," I say with a shrug.

"You would think that." With that she stands, wipes her eyes quickly and starts to walk past me. I don't let her. Pressing my hand to her stomach, I shove her back a few steps. Our eyes connect and I see something dark in hers. Something she doesn't want anyone to see.

"What should I think? I saw you kiss my brother's girl after you nearly dry fucked them all."

"Fuck you," she sneers. She starts to move once more when I move faster. Slamming her against the wall, I lean into her space.

"You couldn't fuck me if you tried," I hiss, letting my fingers slowly run down her neck to her collarbone. She freezes when I slip my other hand between her thighs. She's wearing a tiny leather skirt that left very little to my damn imagination. I slide my hand slowly up as her breathing picks up.

"I could say the same to you," she says softly. So softly, I nearly missed it. But then I smirk, running my fingers over her soaked panties and groan.

"Then you'd be lying. You're wet, Liz."

"Not for you, I'm not." I like her. She's a challenge. One that I'm willing to take. I slowly lower myself in front of her, pulling her skirt up her thighs. I wait for her to stop me but she doesn't. Slipping her panties to the side, I lean in and give her a long lick. Liz's hands find my hair, tugging and pulling as I lick at her sweet pussy. She rolls her hips, trying to get me closer. I slide a finger inside of her and nip at her flesh.

"Fuck," she hisses. I can feel her body tightening. She's so close to coming but I won't let her. Instead, I pull my finger free and stand quickly, pressing my wet lips to hers. My tongue dives into her mouth against her protest but she quickly calms and kisses me back. When she's panting, damn near begging for more, I move. Her eyes are lust-filled and dazed as she stares at me. I smirk knowing I'm not going to give her what she wants. That's when she surprises me. Her hand slides down her stomach, pulling her skirt up her hips. Her fingers dip inside of her as her lips part. She pulls them free and circles her clit. She's panting, moaning and then she's coming in a wave as she leans against the side of the building. My cock pulses in my jeans as I watch the fire in her eyes. What is with this girl?

Stepping closer, I grab her hand and jerk it free from between her legs and bring it to my mouth, sucking her fingers clean. I nearly growl at the taste of her on my tongue. This girl infuriates me for a reason I don't even know, but I can't stop myself from wanting to taste her, touch her.

"Good thing you can please yourself," I say as I drop her hand.

"I know. I don't need a man to make me feel alive." She adjusts her skirt and walks away as I adjust myself and follow. Danny comes out and observes us, a lazy grin on his face.

"What's going on?"

"Nothing. I'm heading out. You might want to keep an eye

on that one," I say, nodding toward Liz. She flips me off and walks back inside as Danny laughs.

"She's a handful," he says.

"I can see that."

"She isn't a toy, Knox. I get it, the way you are, but she isn't the girl to play games with. She's got a lot on her plate right now." I cross my arms over my chest. I don't like being told what to do.

"Like what?" Now I'm curious to know what she has going on.

"Not my business to say." Just as the words leave his mouth, shots can be heard. Screams echo as people run from the building. This cannot be happening again. I rush past Danny and start shoving people out of my way to get back inside when I find Steele.

"What's going on?"

"I don't know. Someone fired shots," he hollers over the noise. The music is off now, the building quieting down.

"Liz!" Danny calls out as we hear sirens.

"Anyone hit?" I ask, glancing around.

"No. Not that I've seen. Just scared."

"Have you seen Liz?" Danny frantically asks Whisper.

"No. She may have gone outside though. Come on," she says grabbing his hand and leading him through the door. It doesn't take long before the cops come swarming in, Blake finding us immediately.

"What happened?"

"We don't know. Someone fired shots. The club cleared out," Steele informs him. He nods and rambles on about something when Danny comes running back in.

"She isn't out there!" He's frantic.

"Whisper, check the bathroom," I tell her. She nods and takes off as the rest of us break up to search the club.

"She's in here!" Whisper's voice blasts through the open space. Danny takes off as I lean against the wall and wait.

"Well that was one hell of a reopening," Callan chuckles, leaning in next to me. Blake's off talking to Leddy as I assess the club.

"This doesn't have anything to do with us this time," I say out loud.

"Sure as hell hope not. That would mean someone is coming back from the dead," Steele adds with a pissed tone.

"It's not us," I say once more. I shove off the wall and head toward Leddy when Danny comes out.

"You still have a doctor?" I hear him ask Steele.

"Yeah, why?"

"I need a favor," Danny says. That catches my attention. I turn around and stalk back toward the bathroom wondering what the hell is going on now. When I step in, I see Whisper kneeling next to Liz. Liz's eyes are vacant, like she isn't even here.

"What the fuck is going on?"

"She's not okay, Knox," Whisper says just as Liz's body begins to tremble. I move toward her, kneeling next to Whisper, waving my hand in front of Liz's face. She doesn't respond.

"Well that isn't good."

"Great observation, asshole! Get her off the floor!" Whisper snaps. Without overthinking it, I reach for her and lift her in my arms carrying her out of the bathroom.

"She's just in shock," I announce as I walk out. Danny is at my side in seconds.

"You don't get it. This is bad."

"What don't we get?" Steele asks as Callan walks up.

"She's running. Fuck! I shouldn't be telling you this."

"Spit it out, Danny. If you want our help, you better open your mouth," Callan growls.

"Liz witnessed a murder. They knew she saw them. She's been running for months now."

"Whose murder?" I ask, glancing down at the trembling girl in my arms before peering back at her cousin.

"Her mom's. The guy, he was a drug dealer that knew some of the cops." Well that changes things.

"We aren't getting involved," Callan states as simple as that. Steele looks to me and then the girl in my arms before slowly lifting his gaze once more.

"What?"

"Your call," he says causally.

"Why the hell is it my call?"

"No. We're not risking Whisper, Shane or Bella for this girl. We don't know shit about her!" Callan snaps. He's been like this since he and Shane got Bella back. I can't say that I blame him either.

"How do we know that's who fired the shots?" I ask, looking between everyone. When no one answers, I nod. "Exactly. There's nothing for us to get involved in. Let's get the hell out of here before Blake starts asking a hundred questions that I don't feel like answering." With Liz in my arms, I walk out the front door and straight to my truck. I heft her shocked body into the back as Danny climbs in the front. This night has gotten a little strange.

8

———

LIZ

He sits there with his feet kicked up on the table in front of him, a drink in his hand. He doesn't glance over at me, just stares straight ahead. I'm worn out, my body aches as if I've been run over by a truck. My head pounds and my stomach turns as I think about what happened at the club.

"Don't fucking throw up on my bed," Knox says without looking over. I don't know how he even knows I'm awake right now.

"I won't." I start to sit up when his eyes turn in my direction.

"Don't do that either. Doc gave you some meds." I ignore him and try to sit up anyway when the room spins faster. Bile races up my throat and explodes from my mouth. "Goddamn it, I said don't throw up on my bed." Knox swallows down the rest of his drink before setting the glass on the table. I try to move, to clean up or do something, but his large hands wrap around my waist before I can think and he lifts me off the bed. He carries me into the bathroom, setting me on the edge of the bathtub before he retreats back into the room. I slowly slide off the tub and onto the floor, crawling toward the toilet. Everything hits me at one time. The shots. The memories. The visions. I'm hanging over the toilet when Knox walks back in. He's mumbling under his breath as I heave. He moves around me as if I'm not even in the room, grabbing clean sheets and walking back out. I rest my face on my hand, thanking God that he's a clean person and there isn't piss stains all over.

"Are you going to kiss my fucking toilet?" His anger pisses me off.

"I didn't ask to be here," I remind him as I drag myself away from the toilet and to my feet. Knox moves to turn the sink on, pulling a new toothbrush from under the sink and holding it out to me. I take it but don't smile. Instead, I grab the toothpaste and brush my teeth while he leans against the doorframe watching me. When I'm finished, I turn to face him fully, noting how big he appears in the small frame. He's imposing to say the least.

"You have enemies," he says, waiting to see if I respond.

"Don't we all?" I start to walk past him but he fills the doorway, blocking my exit.

"Not the kind that shoot at us," he says smugly.

"Really? That's not really what I heard." He steps closer to me, invading my space, and I try to inch back but my ass hits the counter and I'm stuck. Knox leans in, resting his hands on either side of me, caging me in.

"What have you heard?"

"Things."

"What things?" he growls.

"That you're all a bunch of entitled assholes. That you're the biggest bullies in this city and that you think you can have everything your way," I snarl. "Am I right?" His eyes crinkle at the sides as he leans down so close I can nearly taste his lips.

"No, but if I want something, I get it. There's no question about that part." The way he says it makes my heart leap in my chest.

"What do you want?" He pulls one hand around, bringing it to my face before slowly running his fingers down my cheek. I suck in a breath, the heat spiraling through me.

"Not you." He steps back, turning and leaving the room as I try and catch my breath. Then I move. I grab my shoes and slip them back on before walking out of his room and down the stairs. That's where I find Whisper.

"Hey, you look better," she says with a smile.

"I feel better, thanks."

"She isn't staying!" I hear someone roar from the other room. Whisper rolls her eyes and grabs my arm, dragging me along with her.

"I think I should get going," I tell her. She laughs and keeps walking.

"What should we do? Throw her ass out on the street?" Steele roars.

"She has a home!" Callan reminds him.

"He's right. I do," I say when Whisper pulls me into the kitchen. She moves around, grabbing a mug and some toast, setting it on the counter and nodding for me to follow. Just as I'm about to, someone or something hits me in the back of my legs. I lower my gaze to see a little girl smiling back at me.

"Hi."

"Hey," I say smiling down at her.

"Bella, where's your mom?" Callan asks her in a calm tone. Not the same one he was just using to talk shit about me.

"In your room, Daddy."

"Daddy?" It slips out before I can stop it as my eyes find Callan's.

"Bella's his daughter," Steele fills me in. I nod but don't say anything further.

"She's beautiful."

"Yeah, thanks. You can't stay here. We don't know you and we don't know who the hell is after you," Callan adds. A slight shudder runs through my body as I swallow hard.

"I didn't ask to stay. I'm going home." With that, I turn on my heel and start to walk away when a hand wraps around my wrist yanking me back.

"I don't think you are. I think you're going to stay right where you are." I'm shocked when I look up and see it's Knox saying those things.

"Who the hell do you think you are?"

"Your new fucking boss," he growls, squeezing my wrist a little tighter.

"You can't keep me here," I remind him.

"Watch me."

"I'll fight," I tell him with my teeth clenched.

"I like her," Whisper says with a laugh.

"Yeah, she's great," Steele chuckles.

"I'm leaving." Jerking my arm away from Knox I head toward the door. It takes seconds for my arms to be thrust behind my back and something cold click into place.

"Are you kidding me?" I squeal as I turn and face the smugness on Knox's face.

"No. I don't like to joke."

"Then what the hell do you think you're doing?" I snap, trying to tug my wrists out of the cuffs.

"I don't know, I think it's a little sexy," Knox says, eyeing me up and down.

"It won't be so sexy when I slit your throat!"

"See? Now I think that's just as sexy. That fire in your eyes. I think you like me, Liz." My mouth falls open as Whisper laughs.

"You are the last person on this earth that I'd feel anything for," I tell him. Knox steps closer, leaning down so he's face-to-face with me. My stomach knots when his lips touch mine. I don't want to respond, I don't want to let him in but damn it, there is something sexy about this bossy fucker and I can't help myself. My lips slowly part and his tongue sneaks in. Just as I'm about to kiss him back, he pulls away chuckling.

"I can smell you," he whispers before stepping back.

"Are you done?" Callan asks, pulling everyone's attention.

"Just having a little fun," Knox tells him, crossing his arms over his chest. I don't think this shit is fun, not even a little.

"Take the cuffs off her and get her out of here!" Callan roars. Steele chuckles before moving to stand in front of him, eyeing him.

"Since when do you own the world? Huh? Since you dragged Shane back here?" Callan's eyes are wild as he stares at his brother.

"Things are different now, Steele, and we all know it."

"No, nothing's changed, Brother. Just your fucking attitude. You need to calm down before you start shit you can't finish."

"It's fine. We're leaving," Knox announces. Whisper spins to peer at him, Steele glances over his shoulder and I huff.

"Where exactly are we going?"

"On a vacation."

9

KNOX

Drunk. That's what I am. I'm fucking drunk. Coming to the cabin might not have been the best choice, but we both needed an outlet. Liz sits in the chair next to the fire with a bottle in her hand and the other cuffed to the chair.

"Why do I need to be here?" she asks, glaring at me.

"Well, for starters, no one wanted you at the house," I remind her.

"I didn't ask to be there to begin with. I have an apartment."

"Yeah, Danny wanted you out of the way until Sheriff Assfuck finds out who was shooting in the club and why," I tell her. There's something about her, I don't know what it is, that just calls to me. I want to hurt her and I want to fuck her. I want to see what she sounds like when she's calling my name with me deep inside of her. *That's not what we're out here for,* I think, shaking my head.

"Why here?"

"It's isolated. No one comes out here," I say, taking another long pull from my beer. Liz looks away, out into the nothingness that surrounds us.

"It's quiet."

"That's the point, princess."

"Why did you need the break?"

"None of your damn business." She sighs and shifts in her seat when I pull out my phone and turn on some music.

"I saw what they did to her," she says softly. I don't know if she's talking to herself or to me, so I turn the music down and shift in my chair.

"Saw who?"

"They were drug dealers. She used a lot, my mom. She owed them more than anyone knew. I had just gotten home from work and I heard them arguing, which wasn't anything new, but then I walked around the corner and I saw him shoot her." Tears fill her eyes. Where we killed our dad, she didn't want to lose her mom. She was taken from her.

"Fuck," I grumble before I move to uncuff her arm.

"They turned and gazed right at me. They knew I saw."

"What did you do?"

"I ran. I never looked back. I knew what would happen to me if they found me. They aren't just some lowlife dealers," she says, keeping her eyes anywhere but on me. My stomach clenches as I let it all sink in.

"And they never found you?" She shakes her head as I turn up the music. Tipping my head back, I let it all fade as the music slowly works its way through me. When I peer up, Liz is on her feet moving to the beat.

"You're not bad," I say, trying to be friendly. Fuck me if I know why.

"Don't try to be nice to me, Knox. It's not our thing." Setting my bottle down, I climb to my feet and move to stand very close to her. I reach out, grabbing her hips in my hands, jerking her closer.

"What is our thing?"

"You being… you." My lips slowly trail a line down her neck as I listen to her sigh. I could get lost in this girl or I could make her life a living hell. I'm a little on the fence right now as to which I want to do more. The way Liz presses her body against mine, well, that makes me think we're on the same page at the moment. Moving my lips to hers, I kiss her roughly before forcing my tongue into her mouth. She takes the bait. She opens up to me and that's all I need. I kiss her like it's my last kiss, my last breath and she lets me, so when I reach down and pull her ass into my hands, I know she won't stop me from doing that either.

"What are you doing?" she whispers as I lift her into my arms. This isn't going to be a love fuck. No, this is going to be a hate fuck that I will enjoy.

"You ever heard of hate fucks?" I carry her toward the porch when she tries to pull away from me. Nice try.

"Let me go," she nearly growls.

"Not a chance in hell." With that, I slam her back against the side of the cabin and crash my lips against hers once more. Liz is franticly kissing me back like a girl possessed yet hates the idea of me fucking her. I think it's the cutest of conundrums. I slowly lower her to her feet before pulling my mouth away. When I go for her pants, she puts her hand on mine to try and stop me. I gaze up, raising an eyebrow and waiting for her to challenge me. When she doesn't, I shake my head and chuckle before getting back to work on her clothes. Once she's naked from the waist down, I drop my jeans, roll on a condom, and lift her once more.

"This is a bad idea," she says softly as I line myself up.

"The worst fucking idea I've ever had," I add as I thrust into her. She cries out but I don't stop there. I buck my hips as I fuck her against the side of the cabin.

"We shouldn't be doing this," she says on a long moan.

"Not at all," I respond as I thrust harder. Anger eats away at my insides as I take her as roughly as possible. I don't know what it is about this girl that pushes my buttons and at the moment, I don't really care. Leaning down, I suck her flesh into my mouth, sucking hard so that it leaves a mark. My mark. Everyone will know that I was inside this tight little pussy of hers. Each one of her whimpers makes me harder. Each time her fingers dig into my shoulders makes me want to hurt her more, and when I pull back and look into her eyes, she's crying.

"Cry for me, Liz." Her eyes jerk to mine as tears stream down her face. I raise one hand and grab her jaw roughly before kissing her again. Fuck, her tears are doing something to me—something dark and feral. She shouldn't cry for me. That's a huge fucking mistake because now that's all I want to see. I pull out of her quickly and drop her on her unsteady legs.

"Turn around," I growl. Liz looks up at me, tears still flowing as if that would stop me. "I said turn around." The thunder in my voice startles her but she turns. I grab her hips, pulling them back toward me before sliding back in. "You better hold on to that wall." Her hands go up, instantly holding herself up as I drive into her over and over. She's so tight, so perfect, which makes me hate her more. She reminds me of *her* and that pisses me off. She can't be like Nina. She can't be.

"You're hurting me," she cries as I dig my fingers into her flesh.

"A little pain never hurt anyone," I tell her as I thrust harder, deeper. Each slap of our bodies together has my balls burning. I finally give up and release, growling the whole time. When the pleasure subsides, I pull out of her and yank my jeans up. Liz stands there, not moving as I walk past and inside the cabin. I head into the bathroom, pulling the condom off and tossing it in the trash. When I stand in front of the mirror and view myself, I don't know who I am anymore. I don't know if I ever really have. Not after her. Not after Nina.

10

LIZ

I've let him fuck me more than once. Maybe I need the release. Maybe I'm just stupid and naïve. I honestly don't know anymore. I don't like him. He doesn't like me. He made it very clear that all it was, was hate sex. It wasn't a lie. He's barely spoken to me at all since we've been here. Two days of near silence is almost unnerving. It's given me too much time to think and I hate that. I don't want to think about them, him. What he did to her. I lied. I told Danny what I wanted him to know. I couldn't tell him the truth. Our family was fucked up anyway and that would have just been another blow I wasn't ready for. So I lied. Not like it matters now. They may know where I am. Where I live. I drop my head into my hands as I listen to Knox yelling on the phone. He's been doing that a lot the last two days. It's different. He's different. After that first phone call, he's looked at me differently. Strangely. If I didn't know any better, I would think that he knew, but there's no way possible.

I jolt when the door slams and he comes stalking in. He paces the floor in the living room while I watch from my place on the couch. He doesn't look at me, just tugs at his hair. I wonder if I should ask what's wrong, but do I really give a shit?

"That's annoying," I say instead of asking what the problem is.

"Did I ask you?" His blue eyes turn my way and I nearly shiver from the glare. This is Knox Alder. This is who he is. I can see it in his eyes. He's dark, evil, cruel.

"No, but I also don't give a shit. Can't you do that outside?" Before I can look away, he moves. He's in my face, dragging me off the couch before spinning me in his arms. With my back pressed to his front, it's hard to breathe. His scent surrounds me, closing me in.

"You're in my cabin. Out here, I can do whatever I want, be whoever I want." His words are a threat, I can hear that much.

"And who do you want to be?" I risk his wrath by asking but I also find myself intrigued by him.

"Who do I want to be? Me. I want to be me again. The man I was before *her*! The man that knew his path in life, not the man that's lost and yearns for something that can never be."

"Who was she?" His hands stay on my waist, gripping me tightly. I know I'm pushing for answers that he doesn't want to give, but maybe, just maybe, I need to hear his reality to face my own.

"I didn't love her. I loved the idea of her. Nina. She was mouthy and beautiful. A lot like you," he says in a low soft tone. He thinks I'm beautiful?

"What happened to her?"

"She was a selfish bitch! She took a part of me when she killed herself. She ruined everything we could have had, could have been and for what? To rot in a fucking grave!" he roars in my ear. I flinch and try to pull away but he doesn't let me. He slowly runs one of his hands up my stomach until stopping at my throat. At first his fingers are gentle but then they slowly wrap around my neck and squeeze.

"Knox?"

"You know what I hated the most?" he asks and I shake my head. What is he doing? Why is he doing this? "I hated that she just left the way she did. That she decided that she was better off dead than with me. Do you know how that fucks a person's head up?" Again, I shake my head as best I can when he squeezes slightly harder. He lowers his head, his lips near my ear. I can feel the warmth of his breath as it dances over my flesh.

"Please." What am I asking for? Him to stop? Him to keep going? I don't even know what I want.

"Please what, Liz? Please let you go? Let you breathe? Or please don't stop?" I don't know the answer to that. His tongue comes out, tracing the shell of my ear when I gasp. Knox chuckles darkly before sinking his teeth in. "I will never let another woman break me like that again." With that, he releases me and storms down the hall. I watch him go as my body trembles. Don't ask me why I'm trembling either because I have no answer. I don't know if that's fear or lust that slips through my veins but either way, I like it.

Dropping back onto the couch, I close my eyes for a few minutes when he comes back. I don't open my eyes to look but I can feel him, feel his stare. It penetrates the darkest of the dark.

"We're leaving."

"Already?"

"You want to stay? Do you think I'd fuck you a little more if we did?" Now I do open my eyes and peer up at him. He's devastatingly dark and gorgeous. He's the most beautiful devil I've ever seen.

"No. I think I've had plenty of that. When are we leaving?"

Aggravation seeps into my pores as I shove to my feet and move toward him. The way his eyes follow me causes a shiver to run down my spine.

"So quick to get away from me?" he asks, raising an eyebrow.

"Oh, I'm sorry. It's not you. You've been such a joy to be around," I add sarcastically.

"Do you know what bothers me about liars, Liz?"

"No, but I'm sure you're going to tell me," I say.

"That they lie to the wrong people. They lie to the ones that could have helped them. Maybe they didn't see that to begin with, or maybe they were just too stupid to realize what was in front of them."

"Why are you telling me this?" I ask, crossing my arms over my chest. Why when he looks at me, does it feel like he's talking about me? Why can I feel a cold invisible hand wrap around my throat? Knox brings his hand up to his face, running his thumb and forefinger along the scruff that lines his jaw as he stares at me.

"You're a liar, Liz."

"No, I'm not." Yes, I am.

"Poor Danny. I mean, here he thought he was keeping his sweet little cousin safe. Putting his life at risk for you and the best you can do is lie to him," he says, sounding sick to his stomach. The look in his eyes is anything but. They're dark, menacing, and fuck, they pull me in.

"I haven't lied to him about anything." The smirk that tugs across his face is even more sinister than the look in his eyes.

"We both know that's not true, Liz," he says, stepping toward me. I step back. What the hell does he know?

"You don't know shit," I hiss.

"What if I do? What if I know all the little secrets that Danny doesn't?" He cocks his head to the side and stares at me, waiting for me to say something more. I open my mouth but nothing comes out. He doesn't know. He doesn't know the truth and if he did, what's the point in hiding it?

"Your gaming skill is lacking, Knox." What am I doing?

"Is it? I thought I was playing it pretty well." Another step toward me and my heart hammers in my chest. Knox reaches up, his fingers running down my cheek as he stares into my eyes. It's too much, he's too much.

"You're losing," I inform him. No, I'm pushing him. I want him to break and tell me what this is all about. I want him to snap and if he knows anything, I want to hear what. I don't like the impending feeling of doom that I got when he said that. His hand slowly slips around the back of my neck before knotting in my hair. He jerks hard, my head snapping back at the force. A loud gasp escapes me as he leans down into my space, licking his lips.

"I never lose, Liz. Ever. And this right here, this thing with you and me? I'm going to ruin you. Break you, and all that you'll be able to do is cry for me." His threat is clear as day. His lips crash into mine before I have the chance to respond to that, only this time, I don't kiss him back. Not that he cares. He keeps moving his mouth over mine until my lips feel bruised and he pulls away.

"Get your shit." With that, he turns and walks away leaving me breathless and unsatisfied.

11
———

KNOX

Nine Inch Nails' song *Closer* is playing loudly through the speakers. Leddy has her hands in the air, her body rolling to the beat. My eyes follow her moves as she spins and comes toward me slowly. I lick my lips watching her body move. If Leddy wasn't such a good friend, I'd fuck her, especially with a body like that.

Sweat drips down my temples as she steps into my space. Gripping her around the back of her neck, I pull her closer. My hips jerk while her body sways, pressing against me. Our dance is sexy as hell. Practicing for our upcoming show has taken a lot out of me but I wouldn't have it any other way. At first, I didn't want to do this with her. I didn't want the bullshit that comes along with Leddy and my brother. She has had feelings for Steele for a long time, but when she asked me to help her break him and Whisper up, I lost my shit a little. She apologized, which is the only reason I'm here right now.

With the flick of my wrist, her body tumbles to the floor and I move to fall on top of her. The music is thundering through my veins, heat coursing through me. I roll my hips while they're between Leddy's legs. She wraps them around my waist as I climb to my knees. Each time she moves her body, I move mine. We're in sync right now. Through music, we both click and that's something that has always amazed me. When I jump up, I release her and she spins away from me. Something must startle her because she stumbles and falls.

"You okay?" I ask, moving toward her.

"Yeah. Just pulled a muscle," she says, rubbing her thigh. I kneel down in front of her and run my hands over her thigh. She sits back and gives me room to work, massaging the muscle. "Shit."

"What?" I ask. She doesn't speak, just nods her head behind me. I turn my head and peer over my shoulder, spotting Liz, Whisper, and Callan walking in. I don't get it until my eyes meet Liz's. Look at her, all pissed off because I'm touching Leddy. I give her a slow grin before turning back to Leddy.

"What's that about?" she asks.

"Just a little fun," I admit.

"Like with Whisper?" she asks, raising an eyebrow.

"Something like that." Leddy huffs as I shove away from her. "You have a problem with me, Leddy?" She shoves herself up off the floor, stretching her leg as she does.

"Yeah, I do. You Alder men and your games are ridiculous. Do you not care how much you hurt them?" she snaps. She's never talked to me like this before. This is new, and it kind of pisses me off. Placing my hands on my hips, I glare at her.

"You forget who funds your bullshit?"

"My bullshit? Fuck you, Knox!"

"Fuck you back, Leddy! You think I need your drama queen act? Find a new partner!" I turn on my heel and storm toward the door, grabbing my bag as I go. I don't see anyone as I throw the door open and walk out. The air is colder now and I welcome it as it hits my skin. That's when I see her. Liz is standing across the street, gazing toward the sky. I don't know what it is about her that pisses me off and screams at me to go to her. It's messing with my head and I don't like it. The last person to do that is dead. I walk toward her, ready to yell at her for no apparent reason when I hear her speak. I didn't realize she was on her phone.

"I'm going home. This is all insane, Danny. I don't need a bodyguard," she says making me smirk. Danny has been on her ass since we came back from the cabin. Nothing panned out with the shooter, at least nothing related to her, but that doesn't mean shit after the phone call I got. Speaking of, I check the time by pulling my own phone out. I have somewhere to be.

I head for my truck, pulling my shirt out of my bag as I walk. Once I reach my truck, I toss my bag in and pull my shirt on peering over at Liz once more. Her free hand flies through the air as she talks to her cousin. Shaking my head, I ignore the annoying urge to go to her and climb in the truck instead. I want to meet this asshole in person. I want to see what kind of information he has on Liz, and I want to see what he looks like.

I start up the truck and pull out onto the road and just as I drive past her, I rev the engine. Liz jumps, glancing over her shoulder, fear on her face. I know why it's there too and it makes me wonder why shit happened the way it did. I suppose we'll find out soon enough.

The drive doesn't take long, seeing how I opted to meet in our town. No way was I going to be stupid enough to step outside of Rolling Springs in the off chance that something could happen. Instead, I pull into the parking lot of the local bar and climb out. Strolling inside, I head for the bar and take a seat, ordering a drink while I wait. That wait isn't long.

"I hear the Alder boys have quite the reputation," a man's voice says behind me. I don't bother to look over, I wasn't the one that called this meeting. I take a long pull from my beer when a guy sits next to me.

"I don't know about that," I respond.

"I do. I didn't come here without doing my homework first." Slowly I turn my head to face the man, and I'm a little shocked when I do. Slightly wavy, dark brown hair sits in a mess on top of his head but the eyes? Those are her eyes.

"And what is this meeting for?" He smiles then, and damn, it's exactly like hers.

"Ah, straight to the point. I want to offer you a job." I snort a laugh and twirl my bottle around between my fingers.

"I don't need a job in case you didn't notice. I own it all," I remind him. His smug smile pisses me off but after what he'd said to me on the phone, I'm interested in learning more about this little situation.

"Oh, I know. This seems to be your specialty though."

"Which is?"

"My sister."

"You said as much on the phone. Do you want to get on with the point of all this or what?" My nerves are wearing thin where this punk is concerned. If he hadn't asked me to meet him personally, and who it was about, I might have blown him off.

"Fine. She saw what I did."

"What?" My eyes find his and a slow grin creeps across his face.

"I assume you didn't know that part," he adds.

"No. That wasn't what I was told." He nods his head.

"I wouldn't have told that part either. Who wants to come right out and say that their brother is a murderer?" he muses, a slight laugh in his words. Is he kidding me? Does he not know fully what we do?

"The point?" I ask once more.

"I need her out of the way, but first I need her to trust someone enough to sign over a few things." Now I laugh.

"Trust? Yeah, you got the wrong guy," I inform him as I bring my beer to my lips and take a long pull.

"Or fear. Isn't that what you're good at? Instilling fear in people?" I swallow thickly as I take him in. I could easily fuck his world up if I needed to.

"What are you gaining from this?"

"I told you, I need some papers signed."

"Yeah, you're going to have to do a little better than that."

"Our mother, she had stocks, bonds, life insurance. That sort of thing."

"A drug addict that had a life insurance policy doesn't seem too legit if you ask me," I tell him, keeping calm although I see the look on his face. He's not liking the way I talk much at all.

"Some things are just better left unsaid." I find his answer amusing and chuckle. Knocking on the bar, I motion for another beer before finishing off the one in my hand and turning to completely appraise him.

"Look, Jeremy. You are making this all more difficult than it needs to be. You want me to do something for you, you tell me what that thing is and don't beat around the fucking bush. Spit it out or get the fuck out of my town," I snarl.

"She didn't use as much as Liz thought she did. I made sure she was high enough when Liz was around to believe that story."

"Why?"

"The life insurance policy is nearly two million."

"Let me guess, that money goes to Liz, right?" I lock eyes with him, wondering what kind of piece of shit he is to kill his own mom for money. I understand we aren't much different in the killing of family, but at least we had a legitimate reason to do so. Jeremy nods his head.

"You're right."

"And you need sister out of the way so you can have it all. Doesn't seem fair to me," I tell him as the bartender sets another beer in front of me. Lifting that one to my lips, I eye Jeremy for his reaction. I like the fire I see now that I've gotten him all pissed off.

"She doesn't deserve a dime!" he roars, pulling attention.

"And why not? Did she not share her toys with you as a kid? Huh?" There it is. That evilness that lurks in us all. Jeremy has it too, just like I thought he did. Hell, he's trying to kill his own sister.

"She's the reason our dad left."

"Oh boohoo. So fucking what, man. Some people are better off without their fathers. You aren't giving me one good reason to help you. You're wasting my damn time," I inform him as I stand, pull some cash from my pocket, and drop it onto the bar. I turn and walk back outside, but I know he's behind me. If it's a fight he wants, I'll gladly give it to him.

"Half."

"What?" I ask, glancing over my shoulder.

"I'll give you half." Now I full on laugh.

"Are you aware that I have more money than I know what to do with? That me and my brothers own this town and everything and everyone in it? I don't need your money."

"Fine. Then you can have her." I bite my lip between my teeth because frankly, I already have her.

"What would this job entail exactly?" I ask just out of pure amusement. I finally turn to face him and see the look on his face. He's just as sick in the head as we are.

"I either need her scared to death and ready to sign it all over, or I need her trusting and happy enough to do the same. Completely your choice on how you go about that," he says. I nod my head and consider what he said to me. I was already playing games with her so why couldn't I go a little deeper? Scare her a little more?

"How long?"

"Three months, tops. People will start sniffing around if they aren't taken care of by then." Running my thumb over my bottom lip, I mull this over in my head. Next week is the last week of school before our Thanksgiving break, then there's Christmas. I suppose fucking her life up a little more wouldn't hurt anything.

"Fine. You stay out of my way while I do it, and I will let you know when she's ready to sign."

12

LIZ

I walk toward my next class, my head in a fog. I'm on edge and I don't know why. I've been back at my apartment for a while now but things just seem off. I can't place it and after seeing Knox with Leddy the other day, everything has shifted. Someone slams into me, causing me to drop my books before they are kicked across the hall.

"Pay attention, Liz. I don't like when little girls get in my way." When I look up, I see the darkness in Knox's eyes.

"How high school of you to kick my books, Knox." His eyes light up as he steps closer to me. I back against the wall, loving that I can evoke some kind of emotions in him, but hating myself at the same time knowing he could break me if he wanted to. His hand comes to rest on my stomach before slowly creeping into the top of my jeans. I move to try and stop him but he stops me first.

"Tell me why every time I do something mean and cruel to you it makes you wet, Liz." I hate him. I want him but I still hate him. His fingers slowly slip into my panties before moving lower. Each caress of his finger against my wetness sends me a little higher. He works my clit, applying pressure as he does and I can't help but arch into his touch. He laughs loudly as he keeps going.

"Finger fucked in the hall at school is a little inappropriate isn't it?" he says loud enough to draw attention. A few guys walking past laugh, a few girls stare. I push at his hand but he doesn't move. He just inches closer, pressing his chest against mine as he rubs harder, faster. Leaning down, he licks my lip. I turn my head trying to get him away from me but his free hand comes up, gripping my chin roughly before he bites down into my lip. A scream rips from my throat before he pulls back laughing even harder. As fast as his hand went into my pants, they are gone and I'm left flushed and horny, in need of a release. People are laughing and staring as embarrassment rips through me. Knox walks away, licking his fingers as he goes, looking as smug as always. I take a deep breath and will the anger and hurt to go away before class. At least I will have Whisper in dance.

Sucking in a lungful of air, I walk toward my books and gather them up before heading to class. Once inside, Whisper spots me and comes rushing toward me.

"Hey! I've missed you. Why haven't you come by?" My eyes move from hers to Knox and back. She follows and rolls her eyes. "Don't let him get to you."

"He's not. I just need to find a new job and everything."

"Oh that's easy. You can work at the studio."

"The dance studio?" I ask.

"Yeah. Why not? It's fun and I'm usually there when I'm not here," she says, grabbing me and pulling me across the floor. Music comes over the speakers and before I know what's happening, Knox and Callan are in the middle of the room. They are standing facing each other, smirks on their perfect faces. I drop my books and backpack next to Whisper's as I turn and watch them.

"What's this?" I ask her as they both start to move.

"Teacher isn't here. Instead of canceling class, those two thought it would be fun to take over. God, could it be any hotter?" I have to laugh at her. She's with Steele but that doesn't stop her from ogling those two. They both roll their hips and jerk to the sides when they reach over their shoulders and pull their shirts off. Tossing them to the side, Whisper screams. She isn't the only one, either. The other girls in the class practically pant over them while the guys all look envious. I lick my lips as Knox drops to the floor and rocks his hips. Why does he have to look so damn sexy doing that? And in class at that?

"Shit, that's hot," Whisper says, causing me to laugh once more. Callan spins, motioning for Whisper to come to him. I'm almost shocked when she goes but then again, this is Whisper. Callan pulls her into the middle of the room and Knox moves in on one side. The dance is hot, sexy and erotic. Out of the corner of my eye, I see another girl start heading for the middle. My eyes follow her as she steps up next to Knox. She lifts her hand, resting it on his shoulder before he turns and looks at her. He says something that I can't hear over the music before nodding and turning toward her. Except, his eyes don't stay on hers. They stay on me.

Knox rotates his hips, his body pressing against hers. Think new age dirty dancing and that's what's happening right here in front of me. Heat coils inside of me as he thrusts his hips into her. Maybe it's because I know exactly what that feels like that it bothers me. Something inside of me quivers and nearly snaps. What the hell is wrong with me? Surely, I can't be jealous of something that isn't mine to begin with. Can I? Instead of finding out, I walk toward the door with hurried steps. I don't make it that far when hands wrap around my waist, pulling me back.

"The fun is just starting," Knox whispers in my ear. A shiver races through me.

"You were doing just fine without me."

"Maybe, but now I have you here," he adds. I can feel him hard and ready behind me.

"Get off me, Knox," I hiss. He rolls his hips and I moan softly. He laughs, pushing into me further.

"You don't really want that do you?" Grabbing my wrist, he spins me away from him while the class goes insane. Some kind of instrumental club mix comes over the speakers as Knox pulls me back into him. "Move your body." His words are a demand. A demand my body listens to. Slowly, I begin to move with him. His hand wraps around the back of my neck as he dances in front of me but never takes his hand off me. Our eyes lock and it's like all the air in the room has been sucked right out. There's something glimmering in his big blue eyes, something that I want to grab hold of and keep forever.

I duck under his arm and twirl before grabbing his hips and dropping to the floor. Pressing my chest against him, I slowly drag myself up until he grabs me by the hair. Jerking my head back, I gasp as I pant for air. His lips come close, nearly touching the flesh on my neck. I can feel him breathing against me while still dancing. Things are getting hot in here when I feel hands on my waist. I don't even look to see who it is, but the smirk on Knox's face tells me it's Callan. Callan's hands move up close to my ribs as he moves in closer. The feeling of being in between the two of them is almost more than I can handle. Knox releases the grip on my hair and I right my head, looking him in the eyes. There's a serious look there, one that I haven't seen much of. Then he leans down and bites my neck causing me to gasp loudly. The music stops and everyone is cheering. Callan moves back yelling something at them that has them all laughing but Knox and me? We stay in a standoff, staring at each other with so much intensity that I can't think straight.

"I know you like my dick but not during class. I thought I finger fucked you enough in the hall." His words are a slap to the face. My cheeks heat as the words *whore* are thrown around the room. A few girls laugh as Knox winks in their direction. Having enough of this class, I grab my things and head for the door.

"Don't go, Liz!" I hear Whisper. When I don't turn back, she yells at Knox, "You bastard! You need to calm down!"

"It's no different from how we played with you, Whisper," Callan adds. The class laughs but I'm already out the door and heading down the hall when I nearly run into someone.

"In a hurry?"

"No. Yes. I'm sorry," I say flustered by what just took place in there. When I look up, the guy in front of me smiles sweetly, which is a change to the way Knox has been treating me.

"Which is it? And there's nothing to be sorry for," he adds, extending his hand. "I'm Tommy." I reach out and grab his hand in mine.

"I'm Liz. Sorry, I was just coming from my dance class."

"Ah, you dance. Well I'm a professor here. A new one that is and I'm not sure where I'm heading." I almost giggle at the way he says it, but damn, he's not bad to look at.

"Which class?"

"I'll be teaching Art Appreciation. Apparently the old professor fell ill and hasn't been able to return. I don't suppose you're in that class," he says, his eyes roaming my face. I shake my head and brush my hair away from my face.

"No, I'm not but I can tell you, you are going the right direction. It's down at the end of the hall," I inform him with a smile.

"Shame I won't get to see that face every day." Butterflies dance in my stomach as he smiles and walks past me. I turn to get a better glance at his ass when Knox walks out of the dance room. His eyes move from mine to the professor's and back. Something dark takes hold of him, and his hands clench at his sides. Well that's a new one. Instead of giving him what he's looking for, I flip him off and head toward my next lecture.

13

KNOX

I lean back in the darkness and let it surround me. It keeps me hidden from prying eyes but it also gives me cover. I light a cigarette and lean back, watching her window. I can vaguely make out her form as she moves through the small apartment. She shouldn't be there alone. She shouldn't be there at all, but the games that Jeremy wants me to play? This is the perfect place for her.

I watch her shadow as it comes closer to the window, pulling the thin curtain aside. She peeks out as I inhale a lungful of nicotine, just enough so that she can see the glow of the tip. She spots it, her eyes narrowing as she tries to see who I am. I quickly flick the cigarette in her direction and watch as the curtain closes faster than it opened. I chuckle under my breath, but I don't move. I don't want to. In fact, there isn't any other place that I want to be but here watching her. Something about that girl has dug its claws into my chest and won't let go. It's not that I like her that much, I'm not really sure that I do, but the idea of her being my prey sounds awfully good right now.

I sit in the darkness until the lights go out, hell I sit here an extra thirty minutes because I can't bring myself to get up and walk away. When I think it's clear, I shove myself up off the ground and wipe my jeans before walking toward her door. Pulling my lock kit out, I lean down and pick her lock.

Shoving the tools back into my pocket, I turn the handle and step inside. I glance around her small living room before closing the door behind me and locking it. Her scent is everywhere, on everything. I move slowly through the living room careful not to make a sound and startle her. Picking up her jacket, I bring it to my nose and inhale. Lavender and strawberry. That's what she always smells like. Setting the jacket back in its place, I move into the kitchen. One glass sits on the edge of the sink, a bottle of Vodka next to it.

"My little princess likes to drink alone, huh?" I mumble to myself before turning and heading down the small hallway. I can practically feel her. My body knows hers and now it doesn't want to let her go. The closer I get, the harder I become. My heart starts beating erratically in my chest. I don't know how or why she does this to me but I feel it. And I fucking hate it. I hate her for making me have these emotions that I've kept locked away.

Reaching for her doorknob, I hesitate but only for a second. When I push it open, I see her. She's laying on her stomach, one leg curved and stretched to the side. She has on a thong and what looks like a small tank top. That sweet round ass is bare and begging to be touched. I walk closer, careful not to wake her. I can hear her breathing slow shallow breaths. My nostrils flare the closer I get. I don't know what it is that makes me want to hurt her and fuck her all at the same time. My cock is straining against my zipper as I take her in. Her flawless skin, her pure complexion. A soft groan escapes my lips as I inch closer and closer until I run my fingers up her bare flesh.

At first she doesn't move, not even stirring a little, but the further up her thigh I trail my fingers, the more she feels it. Liz starts to groan, slowly shifting her body around. That's when I climb onto the bed. I crawl up her body just as she starts to wake.

I'm faster than she is, moving my hand to cover her mouth before she can scream. My body presses into hers, holding her in place as she silently begins to sob. Fuck, what am I doing? I shouldn't be here; I shouldn't be doing this to her but I can't help myself. I bring my lips close to her ear and breathe her in. I know she can feel my breath dancing along her flesh as she cries. She has her eyes clenched shut as silent sobs shake her whole body. Slowly, I remove my hand from her mouth but keep my body against hers.

"Please, don't do this. I don't know what you want from me." She cries harder.

"I want everything," I whisper. Her sobs slowly start to calm, no doubt from the sound of my voice, but I shouldn't be calming for her. She should be afraid of me.

"How… how did you get in here?" she asks, her voice shaky. That's better. That's what I wanted to hear.

"It's simple, really." I press my lips to her cheek just enough that she can feel them. "I didn't like the way you were looking at that new professor, Liz." Her body trembles.

"What? I wasn't," she begins when I shove my cock against her body. She gasps and closes her mouth as I grind myself against her. It feels so good when I know it's all wrong.

"You were. I saw you. Why do you want to fuck with my head, Liz? What gives you that right?" She doesn't have an answer for me. No one does, not even myself.

"I didn't do anything to you. Get out of my apartment, Knox," she hisses under her breath.

"You would like that wouldn't you? If I just up and left you alone. Do you not remember where you are?"

"Please." Her voice catches slightly but I didn't miss it.

"This is my town. Everything in it, including you, belongs to me," I remind her. I'm not that stupid. I know I don't own everything but the thought of her believing that settles something in me.

"What do you want from me?" There it is. That's what I was waiting for. I climb off her, rolling her onto her back before taking my place between her legs. She tries to kick, but she doesn't get anywhere.

"This. To see you cry for me, Liz. That's what I want."

"You're sick," she says through her gritted teeth as tears slide down her cheeks. I want to lick each one, taste her anger on my tongue, so I do. I lean down and lick a tear as it slips free and groan.

"You are making a big mistake sticking around here. You should run, Liz." I don't know why I want to warn her away, but whatever it is Jeremy has planned for her could go from bad to worse. I like fucking with her head and her body but I don't want to see her dead. Jeremy, on the other hand, doesn't seem to care either way. I have to figure out a way to keep him from hurting her without letting on that I actually give two fucks.

"I have nowhere else to go."

"You've been running haven't you?" Her eyes come to meet mine but she refuses to answer me. It's that defiance that calls to me too. The fact that I can make her cry, but she still refuses to give me what I want.

"I live here now." Slowly, her tears begin to stop and her features harden. This is the girl that has run for months. This is the girl that can hold her head high and not let me have what I want with her. She won't give me her tears because she knows now, that that's what I want. I smirk as I lean down and press my lips to hers. She doesn't kiss me back and I didn't expect her to, but I make damn sure that her lips are bruised and swollen before I stop. When I climb off her and onto my feet, she leaps off the bed and runs. I cock my head to the side and chuckle, knowing she's probably trying to get help. Strolling out of the room and down the hall, I come face-to-face with Liz and a knife.

"What are you going to do with that?" I ask in a teasing tone. It amuses me that she actually thought that would work.

"Get out of here and stay away from me, Knox." Her hand trembles as if she's never held a knife before. I step toward her as she raises it a little higher, pointing the tip right at me. When my chest presses against it, I growl as I feel it prick through my shirt and into my flesh. Liz watches me, her mouth falling open as I look her in the eyes.

"You're not going to stab me, Liz."

"Yes, I will. Get out!"

"No," I say, shaking my head and moving a little closer. The burn is there; I can feel it but I need to make my point with her. "You won't hurt me and we both know it. You want me too much to do that."

"You're insane! I don't want you, Knox. You need to go." Her voice has lowered and when I reach out and grab her wrist, she startles. I squeeze hard enough that she drops the knife before I slam her against the wall. I'm too damn hard for this. My lips crash into hers, nipping and biting. Liz doesn't hold back this time either. Her mouth moves with mine, hell it might be going faster than mine. Our tongues intertwine, slipping over the other as if they were meant to. I grab the buckle on my jeans and pull them down quickly but not before grabbing a condom from the pocket. I step back and tear it open while Liz watches me with wide unsure eyes. I tear it open and roll it on before my gaze collides with hers. We're two wrongs fighting for a right. We're two broken people looking for the wholeness that only another fucked-up human could provide, and it doesn't matter if it breaks me all over again, I'm not stopping this.

"Say no, Liz." She shakes her head and that's it. I lose all sense of control. I move in, slamming her harder against the wall until she bites into my lip. Then I'm lifting her, kicking my jeans and shoes off, carrying her back to her room, and laying her on her bed.

"This is a bad idea," I whisper as I suck the flesh of her neck into my mouth. She moans and arches her back, trying to get me where she wants me. I reach between us, grab my cock and plunge into her. Her screams are music to my ears. I pull my lips away from hers before grabbing her thighs and spreading her wide. Each thrust is harder and faster. I roll my hips, trying to get as deeply inside of her as I can. For whatever messed up reason, I'm finding I need this girl in my life.

I find myself lost in thought more often than not this past week. Is what I'm feeling for Knox real? Is it wrong? How can I want someone that obviously only wants to use me? There are so many questions that I don't have answers for, and I'm not sure how to find them.

"Are you even listening to me?" I glance over when Whisper elbows me.

"What did you say?"

"Are you kidding me? What the hell has gotten into you besides Knox's cock?" she asks with a hint of laughter in her voice.

"It's not like that."

"Yeah, okay. I see how he looks at you. Like you're his next meal."

"He broke into my apartment, Whisper," I inform her. That has her stopping in her tracks. Her face falls and her hands ball in her lap. I know she's about to lose her shit and go off on him, but that's the last thing I wanted to do today. It's Thanksgiving and Steele and Whisper invited me and Danny to go out with them. I didn't want to, but I also didn't want to be alone. Danny jumped at the idea, considering he's friends with all of them too, but then had another friend from out of town ask him to finish up some tat work. He basically ditched me for him. Not that I mind hanging out with Whisper.

"I'll kick his ass," she says, gritting her teeth.

"No, you won't. It's Thanksgiving and we are not doing this today," I warn her. She looks around the empty room before dragging her gaze back to meet mine.

"Are you okay? He didn't do anything stupid, did he?" She sounds so concerned and I love that about her. She cares for others in her own screwed up way.

"I'm fine. Everything is fine," I reassure her. She calms slightly, blowing out a breath before smiling.

"For you. Just today, I will be on my best behavior, but I can tell you after the holidays are over, I'm going to rip his cock from his body and burn it in the fireplace." I start laughing, hysterically.

"I won't stop you!" I laugh harder as she joins in. It's nice to be able to laugh and enjoy myself around her. I've been living day-to-day for so long that I don't even remember what it was like to not look over my shoulder and just let loose.

"I don't know what's going on with you or with you and Knox, but tonight is our night. We're going to dinner, we're going dancing and we are going to have an amazing time getting drunk off our asses." I smile at her because I can't help myself. Being around Whisper opens up a new side of me. One that I like.

"Yes. And God help us if we pass out and fall on our faces," I add.

"You won't pass out if I cut your ass off," Steele says as he strolls into the room. My mouth falls open as I take him in. I know Whisper is right there with me. He's wearing a tuxedo. A fucking tuxedo. My eyes roam him from head to toe and my God, I don't think I've ever seen anything looking as good as him. That is until his brother walks in. Knox is dressed exactly the same and my heart leaps into my throat.

"Why are we going with tradition and wearing this shit?" Knox asks as Callan and Shane walk into the room.

"Because we need one thing that keeps us grounded, even if it is dinner and these fucking clothes," Steele growls. I can't take my eyes off Knox. I knew the man looked good in his jeans that hang just right and those long-sleeved t-shirts he wears, but my God, seeing him in a tuxedo is something out of this world. I glance down at the gown that I have on and I can't even compare. Where he looks like he stepped off the cover of a magazine, I look like I fell out of the local goodwill in the first dress I could find.

"Don't you dare say one word," Whisper snaps at me. I glance over and notice her eyes on me. I nod my head slightly before someone is grabbing my hand and pulling me from the couch.

"You look great, Liz," Callan says, making me blush. Shane smiles brightly as their daughter hugs her legs.

"Why aren't you dressed up?" I ask leaning down to talk to her.

"Mom says it's for big people today," she says softly. I reach over and run my hand over her little cheek as she smiles. A woman, I assume to be the babysitter, walks into the room from the kitchen and Bella runs into her waiting arms.

"Let's go. The faster we get this tradition shit over with, the faster I can get out of this." Knox growls low in his throat.

"You look hot, Knox. Stop your whining."

"Stop looking at my brother, Whisper," Steele warns.

"Why? He's fucking hot, Steele. All three of you are. I feel like I'm in the middle of the sexy men of Rolling Springs photo shoot!" She laughs. Steele grabs her arm and jerks her into his body with a growl that could stop your heart. His lips are on hers before she has the chance to say anything more. The more they kiss, the hotter it becomes. I can't stop myself from looking. That's when I feel breath on my naked shoulder.

"Is that getting you off, Liz? Making you hot?" I start to step away from Knox when his hand wraps around my stomach and he pulls me back into him. His hard, hot body molds around mine.

"Please don't do this tonight," I ask him. No, I nearly beg him.

"Do what? Watch the wetness practically drip down your thighs while you watch them? I didn't peg you for that type of girl but if that's what you want, I'll make it happen, Liz." His words send a surge of heat through my body and I find myself clenching my thighs tighter. Knox's lips slowly move over my shoulder, his tongue dipping out to drag across my skin. My breathing picks up as his hand slowly moves up my stomach and cups my breast in his large hand.

"Knox." I whisper his name not knowing what else to do with myself. He's messing with my head, my body.

"You want me, Liz? Admit that you want me," he says, sucking my flesh into his wet warm mouth. My body practically begs for his touch, for the feeling he gives me.

"Can we go?" Shane snaps sounding annoyed.

"Tell me, Liz," he growls against me. My heart pounds in my chest but the words won't form on my lips. How can I want a man that has done nothing but taunt me and embarrass me? How can I feel something toward him? When I don't answer him, Steele steps up in front of me. His hand comes out, trailing a finger along my collarbone before he looks me in the eye.

"The faster you admit to things, the easier it will be on you," he says, his tone low and seductive. I look to Whisper to see if she's bothered at all by him touching me the way he is, but she stands there with a smirk on her face, knowing these men better than me.

"There's nothing to admit. Your brother is insane. He broke into my apartment, he embarrasses me at every turn, and now you want me to admit that I want him? Not a chance in hell." I don't know how I manage to get the words out with the two of them standing this close but I do. Steele keeps running his fingers up the side of my neck until he reaches my cheek. He cups it in his hand and leans in closely.

"You're making a big mistake." He pulls away and grabs Whisper, leading her to the limo that awaits us. Knox bites down into my shoulder, causing me to whimper before he too pulls away and walks toward the car. I'm left breathless and confused. Callan walks past and then Shane wraps her arm around my waist.

"They are intense, Liz. They don't stop until they get what they want," she says as she leads me toward the car.

"I don't know what he wants from me." Shane laughs a little before she moves to stand in front of me.

"He wants you. Isn't that obvious?"

"No. He's rude, he's… he's an asshole to me." She smiles and rests a hand on my shoulder.

"They do that. Don't ask me why, but they like to be the bad guys, and if you just let him in, you'll see he's different," she says before turning and climbing in. The driver smiles my way as I move to climb in behind Shane. As soon as I'm inside, Knox grabs me and pulls me down next to him. This is going to be a long ride.

15

KNOX

Dinner is going good. I'm surprised that we haven't heard any shit about our dad since we've been here. This was his place. We came here for Thanksgiving every year and the owner personally knew him. He must also know that he was a complete asshole that shouldn't be missed because he is bowing down to kiss our asses tonight. I knew my dad had enemies and people that didn't truly like him but the damn owner of the restaurant? I never thought I'd see that.

"You're tense," Callan says, pulling my attention. I glance over with my glass of wine in hand and wait for him to continue but he doesn't.

"No, I'm not."

"Yes, you are. We can all see it. What's going on?" I look my little brother in the eye; the little brother that has since grown into a man. It was hard for me to imagine Cal with a child but seeing him with Bella, he was born to be a father, unlike ours.

"I'm fine. Just thinking about some things."

"We've never half-assed things, Knox. We do things as a

family," he reminds me. I nod my head and debate telling him about Jeremy, but tonight isn't the night for that. Tonight, we are celebrating in a way.

"Not now. Next week," I tell him, which seems to make him happy. He nods his head and turns back to his food. I glance around the table, watching Steele, Whisper, Shane. And then there's Liz. The girl that fucks up my head. What am I going to do with her? She must feel my gaze on her, she looks up and our eyes collide. My head slowly tilts to the side as I take her in, trying to figure her out.

"Excuse me," she says, setting her napkin on the table and shoving out of her chair. The thought of following her nearly has me getting to my feet, but it's Steele's question that stops me.

"Who is Jeremy Knowles?" My head snaps in his direction, nostrils flaring.

"Spying now, are you Steele?" He smiles that dark deadly smile of his.

"No. Just our general upkeep of records." Sure, that's what it is. Although I know Steele has been very vigilant with everything since we've taken over, so it is possible.

"It's a personal matter," I inform him. Callan coughs before he laughs.

"No it's not. Nothing is personal between the three of us, Knox. What is it?"

"I said it's not nothing." Anger slowly begins to creep up on me. I don't need them sniffing around what I'm doing with Liz or Jeremy. I don't need the extra stress.

"Fine. I'll run his name." Steele nearly growls the words. I roll my head around my shoulders trying to relieve some of the tension when Whisper stands and motions for Shane to follow her. At least she knows when shit is getting heated enough to walk away. "Spit it the fuck out."

"Jeremy is Liz's brother. He wants his sister to sign off on some insurance policy their mom had." I tell him the basics. Steele chuckles and leans his elbows on the table, eyeing me.

"What else?"

"That's it."

"Don't you dare lie to me right now, Knox. We've never done this shit before." His anger is warranted. I'm just treading new waters with Liz, and I'm not sure how to handle it all. I swallow hard and mimic the way he's sitting.

"Fine. He wants her to either trust me enough to sign them or fear me enough that I can make her sign them." Callan lets out a low whistle before chuckling.

"Trust you? Yeah, that's not going to happen," he adds.

"I know that."

"So you're going with fear?" Steele says before shrugging. "It's probably the best way, but what do you get in the end? Why can't he handle it himself?"

"That's the thing. He's the one that killed their mother," I inform the two of them. Steele and Callan share a look before bringing their eyes back to me.

"You're kidding me? He's the one she's running from?" Callan asks. I nod my head and take a drink of my wine.

"Seems mom didn't really have a drug problem unless Liz was around. Jeremy got her all fucked up so that it looked like she did. According to him, it bothered Liz so much that she didn't hang out much at home unless it was to sleep." A part of me hated knowing that. That she had to deal with something like that but the other part of me, the sick, dark part wants to know more. It wants to watch her wallow in her own fears.

"That's a little crazy," Steele says, grabbing his drink and taking down the entire glass.

"It is what it is."

"What are you getting out of this? Surely he didn't offer to pay you," Callan muses. When I don't laugh his laughter stops. "Are you shitting me? He offered to pay you?"

"Yeah, one million dollars. I basically laughed in his face," I tell them.

"Okay, so what then? What are you getting?" Steele asks this time.

"Her." Steele sits back in his chair, crossing his arms over his chest as he looks at me.

"That seems a little redundant doesn't it? I mean, you basically already have her."

"There's something about her, Steele."

"You don't think we saw it too? How much her little attitude is so similar to Nina's?" My eyes shoot to Callan's but I should have known. They are my brothers, they know me.

"We see it, Knox, but we didn't know that's what was messing with you." This comes from Steele as I lean back in my chair.

"I don't think it's even all that. Sure, she has the same attitude but it's different, you know? Liz makes me crazy but I can't figure out why. I would swear it was because of Nina, but deep down, I know that's not true," I admit for the first time to them.

"Then what is it? You actually like her?" Callan asks. I run my hand over my face, exhausted from this whole conversation already.

"I don't know. I like watching her cry for me. I like when she begs me. I like when she doesn't think that I know what she wants. Fuck!" I growl.

"Then what are you doing with her? Why help Jeremy?" Callan asks.

"I like the idea of tormenting her."

"Yeah, right into your bed," Steele chuckles.

"Maybe." I shrug. Is that what I like about it? That I can touch her, feel her fear?

"Well, I think if Jeremy is capable of killing his mom, then his sister isn't going to be an issue to take out either." As soon as the words leave Steele's lips, fury courses through my veins. No one is touching her but me. No one.

16

LIZ

"What do you know about his ex?" I ask after talking with Whisper a little about Knox.

"I don't know much. I wasn't around then," she says when Shane steps closer.

"She wasn't but I was. Nina. She was a little off in the head, if you know what I mean."

"Knox said she killed herself," I tell her, remembering that part.

"She did. She was a druggie. He didn't want to see that in her and tried to ignore a lot of it. He was always so angry though. She would turn to the drugs instead of asking him for help. It made him crazier, if that's possible." She grins.

"That had to be hard."

"It was. The guys tried to help him but he just sort of lost himself. He was hard on himself for a long time, thinking he messed up and it was his fault she did it. He still blames himself," Shane adds. I nod my head because I can believe that part. I saw how he looked when he talked about her. Having enough of the conversation, I look at Whisper.

"Think we need to get back out there before your man goes all caveman and stalks in here?" She throws her head back laughing before she nods.

"Yeah, you're probably right. I just hope this night doesn't drag on. I hate wearing dresses," she whines.

"That makes two of us," Shane adds.

"Well count me in too. This is the most uncomfortable thing ever." The three of us laugh as we head out of the bathroom. We're still giggling when we start past the dance floor. Just then, someone grabs my arm. I nearly jump out of my skin when I turn ready to fight.

"Liz. I thought that was you," Tommy says with a smile on his face.

"Hey, what are you doing here?" I ask as I take him in. He isn't as drop dead gorgeous as the Alder men but he is hot. He's wearing a tuxedo much like the guys have on, except he doesn't have his jacket on. His white button-up shirt is unbuttoned at the top and his tanned skin shows beneath. He looks damn good.

"Me and my sister wanted to try something new for Thanksgiving. It's only the two of us," he says as I watch his mouth. What am I doing? Knox will lose his mind if he sees me talking to him. But what do I care? He's rude and doesn't own me.

"That's nice. This is my first time here as well. Some of my friends invited me along so here I am."

"I'm glad I ran into you. I know it's unprofessional but I was going to ask for your number. I understand if you think it's odd but I—"

"Sure."

"Um, yeah? I'm sure there's some rule about it at school. You aren't in any of my classes though, so that may not be an issue. I just… I don't know, wanted to talk to you, get to know you more." Tommy's words are what any girl would want to hear. He isn't much older than me. I can tell by looking at him, but the fact that Knox is a stalker could cause an issue. Why am I even thinking about him right now? He just wants to torture me.

"I understand. I don't think it'll be a problem either." Tommy smiles and pulls his phone out, passing it to me. I put my number in and pass it back when I feel someone behind me.

"Professor. How fancy seeing you here," Steele says with an amused voice. I open my mouth but there's nothing to say.

"It's a nice place. How is your Thanksgiving, Mr. Alder?"

"It's great. Hopefully it stays that way." I can hear the way he says it and the words are directed at me. His hand comes to rest on my shoulder but I shrug him off. Steele laughs and walks away when Tommy brings his gaze back to mine.

"Steele?" he asks with a questioning look in his eye.

"No! Oh God, no. I'm friends with his girlfriend, Whisper, and his brother's girlfriend." Tommy seems to relax at my words which is almost a little amusing. People begin to fill the dance floor as music plays over the speakers. Tommy smiles and extends his hand, holding his palm up toward me.

"Would you dance with me?" I almost hesitate. I almost say no, but then something inside of me says to do it. I slip my hand into his with a smile on my face and let him lead me out onto the floor. His hands wrap around my waist, pulling me closer as we begin to move. My arms slip around his neck and there is just something about this moment that doesn't feel right.

"So you dance, I know that much. What else do you enjoy doing?"

"I don't dance a lot. It was more for something to do. I don't usually stay in one spot too long."

"Ah, you move around a lot. Do you like traveling?" he asks.

"Not as much as you'd think."

"Rolling Springs is a nice place to live. Great schools, nice people," he says.

"Yeah, my cousin lives here. He owns a tattoo shop."

"Is that reason enough for you to stick around?" he asks. I shrug my shoulders when I feel warmth behind me. I don't need to turn to see it's him. I can feel Knox. Tommy stops moving, his eyes going behind me. I close my eyes and try to tamp down the anger that is slowly seeping into my veins. I hate that he thinks he controls everything. Controls me. When Tommy starts to pull his hands free, I reach down and grab them, keeping them in place.

"We're dancing."

"And now you're done," Knox growls behind me.

"No, we're not." Tommy looks torn as to what to do but I keep my hands on his, not really allowing him to move. I'm sure he could if he really wanted to, but he hasn't yet.

"You want to play this game here in front of everyone, Liz? You want me to make a scene?" Knox's words hold a threat that I know is real. He will make a scene, and it will be me and only me that feels the wrath of everyone's judgement. I slowly release the hold I have on Tommy's hands and let mine fall to my sides.

"I'm really sorry. Thank you for the dance," I apologize. Tommy grins and nods his head, but before he can say anything else, Knox steps around me, blocking my view of him. Feeling pissed off, I spin on my heel and stalk back toward the table where I find Whisper. I drop into the chair next to her and sigh. She knows what's happening, she can see it all.

"Smart choice," Callan says with a grin.

"Was it really a choice?" I snap. He chuckles and looks back toward the dance floor where it seems to be getting a little heated between Knox and Tommy. Neither of his brother's make a move to go intervene. Instead, they watch with smirks on their faces. Assholes. Having enough of all this, I stand and head for the door. As far as I'm concerned, dinner is over. Stepping out into the cool air, I shiver.

"That was smart of you to walk away." Damn it. Why does his voice affect me? Why does he affect me? I want nothing more than to snap his damn beautiful neck.

"Why are you doing this to me? Don't you have other girls you can torture and torment? Why me?" I spin around to face him and instantly he has me pulled into his chest. His lips are like fire as they burn against mine. He backs me up until my body hits the brick of the building, and I gasp into his mouth. The brick scrapes at my flesh but I don't care. All I can feel is Knox surrounding me, dissolving me into a pool of nothing.

His lips move from mine and down my neck, licking and sucking as he goes. His warm breath is a tease against my cool flesh.

"Why do you hate me?" I whisper. Knox doesn't stop.

"I don't fucking hate you." His voice rattles my insides. He doesn't hate me? Then what is all this? Why is he doing this?

"I'm confused."

"Good. Stay that way for a little longer, Liz." Then I hear the word that I never thought I'd hear from him. "Please."

17

___

KNOX

What the hell is wrong with me? Why did I ask her that? Why the fuck did I say please?

"You like her." I flip Callan off as I continue to pace the living room.

"He's not wrong," Steele adds. What the fuck is this? Gang up on Knox night?

"What was the plan with her, anyway? Get her to sign the papers?" Callan asks.

"Yeah, then he'd go away. He'd have what he wants and leave her alone," I admit. That was the idea anyway.

"Think about what you just said, and then think about the kind of men we are," Steele says. I look to him and he raises an eyebrow.

"What?"

"If he's doing this to her, is he much different from who we are?" he muses.

"What are you saying?"

"I'm saying, do you really think that's the end, Knox? Sign the little papers and the murderer goes bye-bye?" Steele growls.

"She saw him do it," Callan adds.

"Fuck!" I scream as I tug at my hair. The girls are upstairs drinking and having a blast, and I'm down here trying to figure out what is wrong in my head.

"Make her stay here where we can keep an eye on her," Steele suggests. I laugh at the same time Callan does.

"That won't happen."

"Make it happen. Look, I get it, Knox. I struggled with what I felt for Whisper too. That shit isn't easy and we all know it. Nina's gone, Brother. There was nothing you could have done for her, but Liz? She's here, man. You feel something for her, and you're just going to throw it away because you're scared!"

"I'm not scared," I say with my jaw clenched. Maybe I am scared. Maybe that's why I'm afraid of letting her get too close to me. No, I'm not.

"Yes, you are. You need to admit that shit to yourself before taking it out on everyone else," he says. That's when I move. I fly across the room, slamming my fist into his face. Steele laughs and comes back at me and the fight ensues. I can hear Callan hollering but I can't make out what he's saying. Adrenaline rushes my system, and I can't focus on anything but the feeling of my fist against bone. This is the sick world we grew up in. This is what we were groomed to do, just not to each other. When I hear the girls screaming, I stop. Steele and I are both out of breath as we look each other in the eye.

"You done? Feel better?" he asks. It isn't a taunt, it's a legit question. Sometimes, it's just better if we fix our problems with our fists. I nod my head as he walks toward me, pulling me into a hug. "We got you, Knox. We're brothers, man." I nod my head when he pulls back and I turn to head up the stairs. I'm halfway up when I hear Steele roar.

"Go with him!" Shaking my head, I make it into my room before dropping onto the bed with my head in my hands. This is a mess. It's all too much to deal with. My door opens and closes, and I assume it's Whisper coming to check on me like Steele told her too.

"I don't need your help, Whisper."

"I suppose that's a good thing." Liz's voice fills the room. Her scent, her… everything fills the room.

"I don't need you here."

"Are you sure about that?" I don't look up at her because frankly the way I feel? I might hurt her too, and I don't want to do that.

"Positive." My jaw is clenched, my teeth grinding. I need to get a handle on myself before I lose control completely. Even with my eyes closed, I know she came closer. I can feel this girl. Her hand comes to rest on the back of my head, massaging lightly. What is she doing?

"I'm sorry," she whispers softly, even though she has nothing to be sorry for.

"You didn't do anything."

"Maybe not but she did."

"Who told you?"

"Doesn't matter. I'm sorry you had to feel that," she says. My heart beats harder in my chest. I don't know if this is the right time to do this or if I'm making a huge mistake, but I have to tell her. I can't keep going on like this. It's ruining me.

"I need you to hate me, Liz."

"I've tried. And I thought I did," she says.

"What do you mean thought?" I still can't bring myself to

look up at her. I hear her sigh, but her fingers keep moving through my hair.

"I don't know how to explain it. I don't feel much of anything anymore, but when I'm with you, hell, just around you, every feeling I have inside of me comes alive. Nothing and no one has made me feel like that." Now I do raise my head. I look up at her standing in front of me like a picture of perfection, one I want to ruin and watch cry, and I can't help myself.

"I need to say something and I don't want you to move. I need to see your face," I tell her. Liz swallows hard and nods her head. "Jeremy contacted me." Her mouth falls open and her hand stops moving. She starts to pull her hand back but I reach up quickly and grab it, putting it back. "Don't stop." It's an order. It came out as a demand and much to my surprise, she starts running her fingers through my hair once more. It's soothing, calming.

"How do you know him?" she asks, her voice shaky.

"I don't. He contacted me and told me he knew about you and I was curious. I went and met him at the bar one day."

"Oh my God. You're going to do it aren't you?" My eyes meet tear-filled ones as I stand from the bed. I reach out, running my hand over her cheek before wrapping it around her throat. Her eyes widen until I lean down into her space.

"Do what?" My lips are so close to hers that I can practically taste her on my tongue.

"Kill me," she whispers. I grin and shake my head. My lips press into hers and I moan. Her salty tears slide down her cheeks, wetting my lips a little more. That's what I want from her. I want to taste her every single emotion on my tongue. I want to taste her fear, suck it all in and take it away from her. I want to breathe this girl in and when I let her go, know that it was me and only me that took it all away from her.

"That's the last thing on my mind," I whisper as my lips skate over her flesh.

"He wants me dead doesn't he?"

"Is that a question that you want an answer to right now?" I'm falling. Hard. And I don't know how to stop myself. Losing myself in Liz would mean losing myself once again, but have I ever really found me?

"Knox?"

"Yeah?"

"Will you help me?" Four words that I didn't plan on hearing fall from her lips, slam into my chest. I lean into her, resting my head on her shoulder in the crock of her neck as I breathe her in. I could be making the biggest mistake of my life right now. I could be about to relive the past, and I can't think of a better way to lose myself again.

"Liz?"

"Yeah?"

"Will you stay with me?" I can feel her body tremble against mine and it makes me smile. She still holds some sort of fear of me but not enough that she didn't ask me for help.

"I…"

"Do you trust me, Liz?" Trust. That's a tough one. I've given her no reason to trust me so far, aside from the fact that everything I've promised to do to her, I have. So, it surprises me when she answers.

"Yes."

"Stupid girl," I whisper before dragging her mouth to mine. This kiss is different. It's rough, it's hard, but it's filled with the trust that she's given me. Maybe she's wrong for trusting me but I can feel it. She isn't holding back and for that, I'm not either.

A knock on my door has me pulling away from her with a slight groan.

"What?" No one answers but the door opens and everyone walks in. Bottles of liquor, chips, and every other random thing you could think of in hand, the guys drop onto the couch across my room while the girls climb onto the bed. I look around at everyone getting comfortable but never letting go of Liz. "Party in my room?"

"Why not? The night isn't over yet, and it seems we have more to celebrate than we thought," Callan says, lifting a bottle in the air.

"Which is?" I ask confused. His eyes move to Liz before coming back to mine.

"Her."

"Me?" Liz asks, pulling away from me. "What the hell do I have to do with anything?" There's my fire.

"A lot actually."

"Fuck you, Steele," she snaps flipping him off. Whisper laughs, bringing her bottle to her lips.

"It's family. We're fucking celebrating family. We might not all be blood but we are our own fucked-up form of it," she adds. As I look around the room at the people that have been here for me, the ones that have had my back in the past and the ones I want by my side in the future, I realize she's right. We are some sort of fucked-up family.

18

LIZ

We're all laughing, drunk and happy. I never thought that I'd be sitting in a room full of sexy men and women that I actually like to be around laughing this much. Knox is leaned back against the headboard, one knee propped up, the other hanging off the bed with me right in the middle. My back rests against his chest and each time he laughs, it vibrates through me. Shane and Callan are curled up kissing but Whisper is straddling Steele's lap, damn near fucking him on the couch across the room. Knox takes a pull from the bottle in his hand before leaning down and setting it on the floor next to the bed. His hands wrap around my waist and slowly begin to knead at my flesh through the t-shirt I have on.

"You like watching them?" he whispers in my ear. I shake my head but that's a lie. There's something erotic, sensual about watching those two. "Don't be ashamed, Liz."

"It's different. Sexy," I whisper through my drunken state. I'm not completely gone but I'm close.

"What does it make you feel?" His tongue drags along my

cheek and I moan.

"Hot. My stomach tightens, clenches. I feel heat all through my body," I tell him. His breathing picks up as I turn my head to look at him. His blue eyes glisten as he looks at me, fire building inside of them. He reaches for my face, turning it back to watch them. Steele has shifted them so that Whisper is on her back on the couch, him positioned between her legs. No one cares that the others are in the room. No one bats an eye. Steele shoves Whisper's t-shirt up before lowering his head between her parted thighs.

"Right now, he's breathing her in. Her scent, it drives him crazy. He's so fucking hard for her and she has no idea. His heart is beating a rhythm against his ribs as he contemplates what he wants to do to her body," Knox says in a low sultry tone. My clit pulses, my body shuddering. How are his words doing this to me? My lips part but I can't find the words to say. Knox's hand slides down my stomach, between my thighs. He growls in my ear when he realizes I'm not wearing panties under this shirt.

"Watch him. Imagine what his tongue feels like as it slowly sweeps over her clit," he says huskily as his finger slowly parts me. Then I feel him. His thick finger strokes my clit and I arch off the bed. His laughter vibrates through my body. I gasp as his finger moves a little faster.

"Knox." I say his name like a plea.

"Watch them," he growls. I keep my eyes on the way Steele is licking at Whisper and the way her hands are grasping her breasts. I know I shouldn't be watching but I can't stop myself. It's sexy. And then she comes. She explodes as she whimpers and pulls his hair. Knox flicks my clit and that's all I needed to come with her. I cry his name as his lips move over my neck. My eyes are closed, clenched shut as I ride the incredible wave that Knox just pushed me onto. When I open my eyes, Steele's dark gaze is latched onto us. Whisper shifts and sits up and before I can think about anything else, Knox is moving. His clothes are off, he's on his back and his hard cock is in his hand. He strokes it as he watches me, waiting for me. Pulling the shirt over my head, I crawl up his body and straddle him. He watches intently as I slide down his length, taking him fully inside of me.

"Fuck," I hear Steele groan.

"Cal?" Shane says as if she isn't sure. To normal people, I'm sure this isn't how they do things but these guys are far from normal. I hear Callan whisper something but I can't make out his words. All I can feel is Knox inside of me. He looks at me, his blue eyes seemingly bluer as he nods at me. Rolling my hips, he groans and I watch his stomach muscles bunch as I move. It amazes me that I can affect the man the way I do.

"Goddamn it," I hear Steele hiss. Then the bed shifts and a large hand cups my breast from behind. I'm about to move but the look in Knox's eyes holds me in place. Steele's large tattooed hand pulls and plucks my nipple as Knox holds onto my thighs. That's when I feel warm breath on the other side of my neck. I don't need to look to know Callan is there.

"Family traditions and all," he whispers as his hand slips over my stomach. What the hell does that mean? Family tradition? I'm about to open my mouth and ask when Callan's hand slips further down. My body tingles, responding to all of them. I don't know how the hell I'm controlling what I feel as everything inside of me pulses. Knox begins to buck his hips, the feeling of him filling me fuller. I pant for air when Callan's finger finds my clit. By this time, my body is already trembling out of control, but the harder Knox moves his hips, the higher I become. I wasn't sure I could come again so quickly but then I feel it building. Steele moves, his lips wrapping around my nipple, his teeth sinking into my flesh. My world explodes out of control as I come so hard, I nearly black out. My body tumbles forward, falling onto Knox's sweaty chest as I try to catch my breath. I hear the chuckles as the others move and then the door closes.

"You okay?" Knox asks, running his hand up and down my back.

"Is that a normal occurrence around here?" I ask, still trying to suck in enough air.

"No, so don't get excited about it either." His hand slams against my ass and I yelp, but I can still feel his hard cock inside of me. I've never had a man with this much restraint before. Shoving myself up, I slide him out of me before slowly moving down his body.

"You don't have to do that," he says, watching me.

"Wouldn't that be rude?" I smirk. Knox shakes his head, a smile on his face as I grab the base of his cock and slowly pump it. I lower my head and wrap my lips around him. I can taste myself and that's not something I'm used to. Lowering my head further, I suck him deeply. Knox growls as his hand finds my hair. I've never thought much about having a cock in my mouth but feeling him now, I can't imagine it not.

I twirl my tongue, tasting him as I move. Knox tenses and before I know what's happening, he's coming down the back of my throat. I'm swallowing as much as I can, but even so, some filters from around my lips. Knox smirks as I pull his cock from my mouth. He reaches down, grabbing the sheet and wiping my mouth before dragging me up his body.

"Not used to that?"

"Not that much," I giggle. Knox sighs and pulls me against him like everything is perfect. In some other world maybe but not ours. Jeremy is still out there. He still wants me dead. There's still a threat and I still don't know what's happening to me. My head is a mess and the whiplash of Knox is making me dizzy.

"I won't let him hurt you, Liz."

"You can't promise that. No one can. Running is what I do."

"Aren't you tired of running? Don't you want to settle down in one place?" he asks as he absentmindedly runs his hand up and down my back.

"I've never had that. I wouldn't know if that's something I'd enjoy or not. I watched her, drugged out of her mind, Knox. She wasn't my mom. She was… someone else. It hurt to see that and I tried to stay away as much as I could. I didn't want to see her like that. Running was what got me through it even back then. Her boyfriends, or dealers, whatever the hell you want to call them, weren't as nice as most guys."

"They hurt you." It isn't a question, he already knows.

"Not like you'd think. They hit me. Tried to sleep with me but they never did."

"She wasn't a drug addict, Liz."

"Yes, she was. I was there," I tell him.

"He did it on purpose. Jeremy. He had her drugged up around you so you would stay away. You were in his way, Liz. That's it," he says softly.

"What do you mean?"

"He wants her life insurance." What the hell? I sit up quickly and stare at him unsure of what to say. I didn't even know she had life insurance. This doesn't make any kind of sense.

"I… this doesn't make sense. I didn't know she had life insurance."

"She did. Two million," he adds.

"Dollars?" I gasp loudly. Knox laughs before shoving himself up the bed and leaning against the headboard.

"That's all he wants." He shrugs.

"He killed her for money?"

"Money, power," he says with another shrug. Then it all hits me. He's just like him. He is no different than Jeremy. I've heard the whispered stories. The ones about them killing their dad. I've heard it all but I didn't want to believe it. What am I doing? What am I getting myself into with him? I slowly shift away and grab the discarded t-shirt, pulling it over my head, then I move off the bed. I can feel him watching me but he doesn't say a word as I turn the doorknob and leave the room. My stomach is rolling and I can't seem to think straight. How did I think he was different?

"Leaving so soon?" Steele asks, standing at the end of the hall with his arms crossed over his chest. His sweatpants hang from his hips, his tattoos on full display. It shouldn't be allowed, the fact that they look this good and are so damn evil.

"You're all just like him," I say. Steele waits, an eyebrow raised when I feel Knox behind me.

"What difference does it make?" I spin around and pin him with my gaze. What difference does it make? How can he even ask me that?

"You kill! You kill for money, for power! You are just like him!"

"I'm not him," Knox says, keeping his eyes on mine. There is no sign of hatred, no sign that he even cares what I'm saying about him right now. Because he doesn't care. Why would he? Knox knows full well who he is.

"You're just like him!" I scream louder. Anger creeps through my veins and I can't seem to stop it. How could this be happening? "What did you agree to do for him?" His eyes stay on mine, never moving. Those oceans of blue hold me hostage, drowning me in their depths. The slow dark smirk that crosses his face should tell me enough and yet I wait.

"Ruin you."

19

KNOX

The needles pierce my flesh as I lie here, staring up at the ceiling. Each one burning less than the last.

"Do you want to talk about any of this?" Danny asks as he continues with the devil tattoo on my stomach.

"Nope."

"She's getting to you, isn't she?" I look at him just in time to see the smirk cross his face.

"She doesn't understand me," I inform him even though I think that's partially a lie. She gets me, she just doesn't want to see that part. I can't say that I blame her. She doesn't want to be a part of a world that is bred on the destruction and the damnation of others. Who the hell am I to blame her for that?

"Liz is different. Always has been," he says, keeping his eyes on my abs.

"How so?"

"She's always liked things her way. She's never really conformed to what others wanted her to be. She likes who she is." That much isn't a lie. She's never made apologies about being herself, and I think that's part of what draws me to her.

"I found things out and some of it is strange to me." I want to ask questions and get answers, but I wanted them from her. Yet, she doesn't want to speak to me. I let her be, let her run back to her little apartment for now but I've kept an eye on her.

"Ask me, Knox. If I know, I'll answer." Taking a deep breath, I blow it out slowly.

"Her brother."

"What? She doesn't have a brother," Danny adds as he continues.

"She has a brother, man. I met the motherfucker. He's the one she's running from. He's the one that killed their mom." The machine stops and when I lower my eyes, I see that Danny is finished. The black devil that stares back at me is amazing. It's exactly how I pictured it.

"That makes no sense," he says, shaking his head.

"I don't know what to tell you. His name is Jeremy." Danny cleans me off and I sit up as he runs his hand through his hair.

"I heard that her mom may have had a kid before her and Liz's dad met, but nothing ever came out of it. She blew it off. To be honest, I was never close with that part of my family. I talked to Liz but we weren't even that close until lately. It just doesn't make sense," Danny says, once more shaking his head.

"I don't know the logistics of it all, but he needs her to sign off on the paperwork giving him access to their mom's life insurance."

"And he came to you?"

"Yeah. The motherfucker called me and asked to meet. Offered me half then offered me her." I can see the anger as it slowly seeps into his pores. His hands clench in his lap before he slowly raises his head to look at me.

"You aren't touching her. I won't let you play with her the way you do all the others." The growl that leaves him makes me laugh. I can't help it.

"Who do you think you are, Danny? Just because I consider you a friend doesn't mean you get to tell me what the fuck I can and can't do," I remind him in a harsh tone.

"When it comes to her? Yeah, I can." Shoving out of the chair, I grab my shirt before turning to face him.

"There's one problem with that theory," I add.

"Which is?" Danny is on his feet now.

"The game has already begun." It takes literally seconds for him to lunge at me. I stumble back and we both tumble through the door and out into the hall. A few people scream, a few of his guys move in to pull us apart.

"You stay away from her!" Danny yells, his finger pointed at me.

"Yeah, I can't do that."

"Why? What is he offering you? I'll give you more!"

"He isn't offering me money, Danny." I try to calm myself as I look around but I can feel her. She walks over and looks between the two of us before focusing on him.

"What do you know?"

"All of it. A brother? Who the hell is he, Liz?" Danny asks, directing his attention to her now.

"We don't have the same dad. He's older than me. It's a long story. He wasn't around much when I was younger but when I got older, he was. He showed up and mom was… happy." Danny runs his hand over his face before dropping his head. "I'm sorry, Danny. I didn't want you involved. I knew that you didn't get along with your family and I didn't want to add to it."

"And him? What are you doing with him?" His head comes

up and his eyes lock with mine. That's when she turns to look at me over her shoulder before turning back to him.

"That's complicated."

"Clearly. He's not a good guy, Liz."

"Fuck you, Danny!" I snap.

"I know what he is and what he isn't. You don't have to worry about me when it comes to him. I can handle myself," she says making me chuckle. She didn't really prove that point when she ran out of my house the other night.

"He's a user, Liz. Come on. His last girlfriend killed herself!" That's it. I shove Liz out of my way and slam my fist into Danny's face. We might be friends and I might like him, but this is taking things too far. He moves to swing back at me when Liz launches herself in the middle of us. She shoves his chest hard enough to make him stumble back a little more.

"Don't you dare say that! You don't know anything about them!" she screams.

"He wasn't there for her, I know that much." That's Danny's response. Fuck this shit. I don't need this. I turn on my heel and stalk down the hallway and out the front door before I let myself fall apart. I roar as loud as I can and slam my fist into the brick wall letting the pain ebb and wrap itself around me.

"That's going to hurt in the morning." I glance over at her but shake my head, pull my shirt on, and turn to walk away. My boots hit the pavement as I make my way down the sidewalk. I need to breathe. I need to think.

"Walking away from me isn't helping anything."

"And yet you ran from me!" I don't turn to look at her but I know she's behind me. When I feel her hands on the back of my shirt, I stop. I spin quickly and grab her shoulders roughly in my hands. "Stop, Liz. Just stop! I can't handle anymore. Don't you get that? You're fucking with my head and I can't stop it." Her eyes widen as she stares up at me.

"Do you think you're not doing the same to me?" Her words throw me off for a second. "You think you're not affecting me? You are, Knox. I just don't know what to do with it. I'm running from one life straight into the same thing with someone else. What's the point?"

"The point is, I'm not him. Our lives aren't the same, Liz. Yeah, me and my brothers do questionable things, but that's the way our lives have always been. We're trying to fix that, make it right. Better. Then you walk in and fuck up my life. You fuck up my head and I don't know what to do with that," I admit to her. Her eyes water as she stares at me, not a single word coming from her mouth.

"Knox, I just don't know what to do." I slowly release her and take a step back.

"Go home, Liz."

"Knox, please." Shaking my head, I raise my hands up to stop her from coming closer.

I'm losing it.

"Go home."

Falling.

"Knox," she says softly.

Gone.

"Go home!" I roar.

20

LIZ

I've known defeat most of my life. At times, I could actually admit to it too, but this feeling in my chest is new. It's not one I wanted and I sure as hell don't know how to make it stop.

"You seem sad." I look up from my book to see Tommy smiling down at me.

"Tired. How are you?"

"I'm good. Haven't seen you much since Thanksgiving. How have you been doing?" he asks happily. I sit back and take him in. The whole man. He seems normal enough. Cute. Educated. So why can't I find myself attracted to him? No, of course it would have to be the man that wants to ruin my life and wreck my sanity.

"I'm okay. Ready for the holidays to be over," I admit. I was never much of a fan to begin with.

"I can understand that. Is sitting out in the cold helping with that?" he chuckles. I smile.

"I just wanted some alone time. It seems everywhere I go, there are more and more people."

"I can take a hint." He smiles.

"I'm sorry. I didn't mean it like that. I didn't mean you…" I begin to ramble when I see Callan. I roll my eyes as he strolls toward us, slapping a hand on Tommy's shoulder.

"We have rules against teachers dating students." His smile is bright but it's also a threat. Damn these Alder assholes.

"We aren't dating," I remind him, closing my book and standing from my spot on the bench. So much for that alone time.

"Good thing."

"I was just stopping to say hi, Mr. Alder. That is all," Tommy adds as if Callan really gives two shits. He doesn't.

"Then by all means, please be on your way." My eyes stay on Callan's while my mouth hangs open. I can't believe the set of balls the three of them have. They talk to people in any fashion they choose and everyone just goes with it. Tommy smiles over at me before turning and walking away.

"Why the hell are you so rude?" I snap as I move closer.

"That wasn't rude. I thought I was being pretty nice," he says with that smirk in place.

"You were a complete asshole."

"And you're the reason my brother is at home drunk off his ass instead of taking his tests," he retorts. Oh no. He is not putting that on me.

"Your brother is a dick. If he's at home drunk off his ass, that's on him." I start past him but I knew he wouldn't let me get far. His hand presses into my stomach, pushing me back a step. Then he counters that move and steps closer to me, invading my space.

"I don't know what the hell this thing is between you two, but I suggest you fix it." He growls low in his throat. I've heard the rumors about these three. I know what they are capable of but the way Callan is talking to me? It's downright scary. His tone is lethal.

"I didn't do anything that needs to be fixed, Callan."

"I think you're lying," he hisses.

"I don't give a shit what you think! You might run Shane's world for her but don't you dare try to run mine!" I shove his hand away only for it to come up and grab my hair. My head is jerked back and my mouth parts.

"I don't run Shane's world. I keep her safe. That is what my brother is trying to do for you. You might think you're tough shit and maybe you are to an extent, but when that big brother of yours comes for his payment, you will be no match for him. Now I know Knox is a hard person to love, but trust me when I say that's all he needs." With that, he releases the hold on me and turns to walk away. My stomach is doing flips inside of me, emotions running wild. This is insane.

"Callan!" I call out to him. He slowly turns to look at me as I chew on my lip. "Give me a ride?" He nods his head and waits as I walk over to him, and as soon as I'm close enough, I punch him in the arm.

"What the hell?"

"Don't you ever pull my hair like that again," I hiss. Callan laughs and throws his arm around my shoulders as we walk toward his truck.

"Some girls need it a little rougher than others, Liz. Just relax and get used to it."

"I don't love him," I say, changing the subject.

"Maybe not yet but you care. That's good enough for me," he tells me. I sigh as we continue to walk when a loud boom sounds behind us. Callan immediately shields me and spins to check behind us.

"What was that?"

"I don't know. Get in the truck," he says quickly, ushering me faster. I climb in as soon as we're close enough and he jumps into the driver's seat.

"That's by the science lab," I say, noting the smoke that is billowing from the building. Callan revs up the truck and speeds out of the parking lot quickly as he calls someone on speaker.

"What?"

"Something exploded at the school."

"What the fuck?" Steele's voice is hard on the other end.

"Call Blake. See what's going on," Callan says before hanging up. I shift my book around on my lap when a paper tumbles out. Bending down, I grab it and set it on top of my book as I gaze out the window.

"Wonder what happened," I say softly.

"Who knows? At least it's Christmas break. We have time to deal with it. Probably some idiot freshman."

"Probably."

The rest of the ride to the house is silent. Callan pulls up and I start to climb out when I glance down. The paper—I picked it up off my desk after my last test today. I unfold it and my heart nearly stops.

"Cal?"

"What?"

"I... this...

"What? Spit it out," he says. I reach over and pass him the paper as I stare at my hands. What does he have to do with any of this? Why?

"You're kidding me?"

"It was on my desk with my name on it but I was late to

class. I sat down and did my test not even paying attention to it until now."

"Guess we know what exploded," he chuckles. Glad he thinks this is funny. I could have died! If I would have seen that shit and went there? When I don't move, Callan's door closes. He walks around the truck offering his hand, helping me on my shaking legs. His hands come up to cup my cheeks, forcing me to look at him.

"Liz? Listen to me. Whatever is happening, we are going to find out, okay?" Do I believe him? Why would he find out? Why would any of them help me? I start to shake my head when Shane appears next to us.

"Everything okay?" she asks. Callan's hands never leave my face as I try to think.

"Liz. I mean it. Nothing is going to happen to you." Callan's voice is firm and I find myself nodding along although I don't know how I can trust his word. "Shane, where's Knox?"

"Drunk in the living room."

"Take her to him." I shake my head, not ready to deal with Knox just yet. Callan lowers his hands and pulls his phone out as Shane comes closer to me.

"I don't want to see him."

"Too bad," Callan snaps, and just like that, the nice Callan is gone. Shane wraps her arm around me and leads me toward the house. I still can't believe that he had something to do with it. Was it just coincidence? Oh my God, was he in there? No, he wouldn't have had time to make it to the lab.

"You okay?"

"I don't know, Shane. I feel sick."

"You need a drink," she laughs. I follow her inside and into the living when I see him. Knox is wearing dark sunglasses in the house, leaning back in his chair, legs spread wide. God, he looks perfect. He doesn't speak or move, but I know he's watching me. I can feel him.

"Here," Shane says, pulling my attention to her. I take the glass of alcohol and down it in one gulp. She giggles and refills it. "I need to go check on Bella. She was coloring. You okay?" I nod my head and tip the glass to my lips once more.

"Day drinking is my thing." Knox's words slur.

"Well today, I guess it's mine." Taking the drink down, I move toward the cabinet and grab the whole bottle. I don't think I will be able to wrap my head around all this if I'm sober.

"There's my girl! Go for the whole bottle." I roll my eyes and uncap it, bringing it to my lips. I take a few good pulls before wiping the back of my hand across my mouth.

21

KNOX

My cock is hard. It's fucking raging as it watches her. Yeah, he's watching her just like I am. She doesn't see my eyes with my glasses on, but she can feel me. Callan has been storming through the house since they got here but I'm too drunk to care what it is he's rambling on about. Now with the joint between my lips, I really don't care.

"You want some?" I ask. Liz peers up, her little head swaying slightly from all that she's drank in the last hour. She nods her head and I nod to the floor. She looks at me confused before I answer her. "Come get it. Hands and knees." Liz flips me off and rolls her eyes as I bring the joint back to my lips and inhale. The music on my phone plays over the speakers in the room as I relax and watch her. What is it with watching her that I like so much? The fact that she doesn't understand why I'm looking? The way she doesn't care that I'm looking? I don't know what it is at the moment, but fuck, I like looking at that girl.

"Stop staring at me, asshole." I chuckle and blow smoke through my nose.

"Crawl to me, baby."

"You are so fucked up. Even more than I thought if you think for one second I'm going to crawl to you."

"What about cry for me? Will you cry for me, Liz?" My words are dark, just like my head is right now. Her eyes come to lock with mine from across the room and there's nothing I want to see more than her tears. I've been keeping up with what's going on at the college through the texts and emails coming to my phone between Steele and Callan. I know why she's on edge, but I sure as hell don't let on that I do.

"Fuck you."

"We've done that."

"So?"

"What is fear to you, Liz?" I ask, taking another puff.

"What?"

"Fear. What does it mean to you?" This is going to be fun. I want to play with her, tempt her. Pulling my glasses off, I toss them to the side as I stand. Pulling my long-sleeved t-shirt over my head, her eyes travel over my abs to the devil that stares back at her.

"That's new," she says softly.

"You like it?" She nods slowly. I twist my shirt and move behind the couch she's sitting on, covering her eyes with my shirt and tying it behind her head. I think she's going to stop me but she doesn't.

"What are you doing?"

"What is fear to you, Liz?" I run my fingers along her neck, up her jaw.

"I don't know."

"Yes, you do. Are you scared of me?" I lean down and whisper in her ear. Her body trembles slightly. "Are you afraid that you should have been in that lab?" She starts to reach for the shirt that has her blindfolded but I push her hands away. My lips caress her earlobe as she breathes a little heavier.

"He was going to kill me."

"Does death scare you?" She nods her head. "It shouldn't. You've seen death, Liz. First hand."

"Her eyes. They were pleading with him. Asking him not to do it," she says through a strangled cry. Liz never got over what she saw her brother do. Witnessing her mom being killed tore a piece of her off and tossed it into the wind. She was never whole after that and I know that much. I want her to be whole. I want her to be who she was meant to be. Liz isn't like us. She's beautiful, smart, powerful. She just has to let that part go so she can see there is more than death in life.

"And you sat there, watching."

"I couldn't look away." She cries harder. My lips move to her cheek, soft kisses.

"Why not? Why didn't you look away?" Her body shakes with each sob that now leaves her throat. This is killing her but that's not my goal. I want to heal her. I want her to heal me. She's the new that can replace all the pain of the old. She's the only thing that has me clinging to what's left of my sanity, and if I don't have her fully, I won't have her at all.

"I thought she could feel me there with her so that she wouldn't have to be alone." The cries, the screams, they burst out of her before I reach up and pull my shirt from her eyes. I turn and leave her sitting on the couch as I head into the kitchen. Dropping into the chair, I lean back and sigh. She's as broken as I am, but she has the power to make it all right. I don't know how. I don't know why and that's pissing me off.

"You okay? Your girl is breaking down in there," Callan says as he points over his shoulder, strolling into the room.

"Who do you think broke her, Brother?" I say with a dark smile.

"Whisper's in there with her. She's going to have your ass," he adds.

"Probably. What did you find out?" He grabs a water from the fridge and twists the cap off, taking down half the bottle in one go.

"It was the science lab. Looks like someone turned the gas on and left it. Tommy is missing in action which seems a little odd to me," he says, catching my interest.

"Gone?"

"Yeah. I saw him with her at the school earlier and then he was gone."

"The note was from him?" Callan nods as Steele stalks into the room.

"Aww, look at my little brothers having some bonding time," he teases.

"Fuck you. I got your bonding time right here," I tell him, grabbing my cock. The guys laugh as Steele grabs his own drink and comes to stand next to Callan.

"What's going on in there?" he asks, jerking his head in the direction of the living room.

"Gave Liz a little reality check." Steele raises an eyebrow.

"What?" I ask in response.

"Nothing. She sticking around?" he asks, I shrug.

"Don't really know. That's not on me," I tell him. He nods his head when Whisper storms into the room.

"What is your problem?" she yells as she gets right in my face. Her hands shove at my chest but I don't move because I'm in the chair.

"If you wanted to touch me, you should just ask. I won't say no," I tease her.

"She's a mess!"

"And?"

"And? And you need to go be with her, Knox."

"Oh, no. That is not something I do. I don't chase women, Whisper. You know that much." Her arms cross over her chest, her eyes narrow at me. Damn, she's one hot little thing.

"But you don't have a problem making them cry?" I shake my head with a smirk on my face. Whisper starts to step toward me when Steele grabs her and pulls her back. He whispers in her ear and she smirks.

"I'm getting some guys for security here at night," Callan tells us. I nod my head, knowing that's probably a good idea.

"Good." Shoving out of my chair, I head toward the living room once more but I don't find Liz there. With a shrug, I head up to my room. I don't know if she left or not, and to be honest that thought pisses me off. I stomp into my room and slam the door when I see her. She's standing in the bathroom with a pair of scissors in her hand. Her eyes are vacant as she looks at herself in the mirror. I walk over and lean against the doorframe, crossing my arms over my chest.

"Why?"

"Have you ever looked at yourself and hated everything you see?" Shoving off the doorframe I step up behind her, pressing my body into hers. Then I lean down, resting my chin on her shoulder as we both stare at her reflection.

"What do you hate?"

"Everything."

"Be specific," I tell her.

"I hate that I'm weaker than I thought I was. I hate that I didn't try to stop him. I hate that I ran. That I'm still running. That I've lied to people that care about me and I can't take any of that back." Reaching for the scissors, she allows me to take them.

I set them on the counter and spin her to face me. Grabbing her face in my hands, I lick my suddenly dry lips.

"What I love about you is your strength. I love that you say what you're thinking and how you feel without giving a shit what anyone thinks. I love that you can still move on with your life even after all that you've lived through." Tears stream down her cheeks, ripping my goddamn soul from my body. I've never felt like this for anyone. "I love that you need me as much as I need you." With that, she loses it. She wraps her arms around my waist and hugs me as she cries. For me. She cries for me.

I hold her like this for a long time, but when she finally looks up at me, I know what I did was right. I may have debated it for a second but now, I see it.

"No one has ever seen anything in me."

"Don't lie to me, Liz. People see it, it's you that doesn't." Leaning down, I press my lips to hers and savor the taste of her on my tongue.

22

LIZ

We're all sitting around the fire that the guys made out back with drinks in our hands. It's nice to see everyone together and laughing.

"Where is your head at, Knox?" Steele asks. I've noticed that he's been slightly distracted all night too, but I didn't want to ask questions. Christmas is coming, and I didn't know if that was something the guys celebrated or how they celebrated. I figured that might be why he's so off.

"I want to take her to see Jeremy." I leap from his lap and spin to face him as the rest of them stare.

"What? Why?"

"Sit down, Liz," he says softly.

"No! Fuck that!"

"I like her," Whisper laughs.

"So we're told," Steele adds.

"Now, Liz." This time it comes out as a demand that I know I should follow but damn him. He threw that bomb out there without a second thought. When I don't move, Knox grabs my wrist and yanks me back into his lap with a huff.

"Now that's taken care of. Why do you want her there? Is he not wanting her dead?" Callan asks. I nod.

"He does. But I think it's about time that he knows I'm not playing on his team. I want him to know that she's mine, not his." His words warm my heart as I look over my shoulder at him. His eyes come to meet mine and I'm a little lost in them.

"I'm…"

"Mine. You heard right." A small smile crosses my face before I press my lips to his. Steele clears his throat, breaking us apart.

"Why does she need to be there?" he asks. I'm kind of curious to know that too.

"I just told you that."

"Do you think he will show with her being there?" Callan asks.

"I don't know. I was going to have her dress down. Hoodie and shit," he says, bringing his beer to his lips and taking a long pull.

"She's your girl, that's on you. We can set up outside just in case, but I doubt he will do shit in public like that. I mean, he blew up the science lab but that wasn't occupied," Steele tells him. His girl. Just hearing it sends a chill down my spine. I've never actually had someone like Knox want me so it's a little strange for me. I'm not sure how I should react and that causes me to tense up. Knox sets his bottle on the ground next to him before wrapping his arms around me as if he can sense what I'm feeling. His strong arms envelope me in a warmth that I never knew existed.

"Speaking of exploding labs, have we heard anything on

Tommy?" Just his name pisses me off. I thought better of him. I thought he actually liked me but that was all a lie.

"Not much. Has a few priors but nothing major," Steele says.

"I want his ass," Knox growls from behind me. I can hear the anger, the rage in his tone.

"And you'll have him." That was Callan.

"Can we get off this depressing subject?" Whisper chimes in.

"What do you want to talk about then?"

"Christmas and how we can spoil the hell out of Bella." Her smile couldn't possibly get any wider and that causes me to smile too.

"You guys already spoil her," Shane states.

"Not enough. It's Christmas. What do you guys usually do?" Whisper asks, glancing over at Steele. He shakes his head and shrugs, running his hand through his hair.

"Not much honestly. Dad was away for most of them. We just sort of hung out and did whatever we wanted," Steele tells her. Her smile fades like everyone else's. I didn't have great holidays but we had a tree.

"You didn't have a tree?" I ask. Knox's arms tighten around me.

"No. Didn't see the need for one," Callan informs us.

"Well, we are having one this year. I think we could all use some holiday cheer." Whisper's smile is huge and her eyes are full of light. I think this might be the happiest I've ever seen her and it makes me smile along with her.

"Jesus Christ, what are we getting into?" Steele hisses under his breath.

"Women. We're getting into women," Callan states.

"Your daughter. She deserves the best of memories with all of you. When she grows up, she will remember every single one," I say softly.

"Liz is right," Shane says. "We don't know what her life has been like up until she came back to us. She deserves that much."

"Don't start the fucking girly crying shit. Bella will have the biggest goddamn tree there is," Knox states. The guys chuckle but the girls? They both beam with happiness. It's the perfect setting for an imperfectly perfect family. I'm about to say more when Knox's warm lips come to rest on my neck. His breath dances over my flesh like the perfect breeze causing bumps to erupt all over my skin.

"What do you want for Christmas, Liz?"

"Nothing."

"Come on. Everyone wants something. If you could make one wish what would it be?" What do I want? My mom back? My brother gone? Happiness?

"I want a home. A place that I will never have to leave. Somewhere that I can call home and truly feel it. I don't want to run anymore, Knox. I'm tired of running. I want to stay in one place and actually make friends and have a life." He doesn't say anything and when I shift in his lap to turn and look at him, his eyes are hard as steel. Something inside of him is slowly coming undone and I don't know if that's a good thing or bad. You never know when it comes to Knox.

"What about you? What do you want?" I take the chance to ask him. He swallows hard, his face softening slightly.

"I want everything. I want your happiness. I want your sadness, your fears. I want it all, Liz. All of you."

23

KNOX

The week has gone by in a blur of bullshit. Liz hasn't left my side and I can't complain about that. I like having her here. I need her here. When she isn't close, I get a sick sense of unease that slithers through my veins. It's not a good thing either. It makes me crazy, crazier than I already am.

"What about that one?" I shake my head, clearing my thoughts away when I hear Bella. I follow her pointed finger to a tree.

"That's too small. Thought you wanted a huge tree?"

"I do, Uncle Knox! How big can I get?" Her eyes widen when I reach down and lift her in my arms. Holding her under her arms, I lift her up into the sky and spin around. She laughs loudly.

"This big! Think you can find one?" She laughs harder as I lower her back to the ground.

"I can do it," she squeals and takes off.

"You're good with her," Callan says stepping up next to me.

"After the way we were raised, how could I not be? I wouldn't want that for her, Brother. She deserves to be loved."

"And you love her?"

"Of course I do. She's my niece."

"I know. I've just never seen this side of you," he laughs.

"Which side is that?" I ask, looking over at him as we follow along behind his little girl.

"The side that actually cares. The side that makes others smile." He's turning into a girl. Bella has this man whipped and wrapped around her little finger. Not that she doesn't have that with all of us, she does, but Callan is different. If anyone makes an amazing father, it's him.

"I care, Cal. I care about all of you, it's just harder for me to express that shit."

"I know but I'm proud of you, Knox." Those words have me stopping in my tracks. I turn to face him, wondering why he even said that to me.

"What?"

"I said I'm proud of you. You're hard as fuck inside and out, Knox, we all know that, but you have something more in there," he says, pressing a finger to my chest. Bella yells that she found a tree and Callan walks off to find her. Whisper moves in, wrapping her arms around my waist.

"What is this for?"

"Nothing. I can hug you whenever I want, you asshole," she snaps. I laugh and hug her back when I see Liz and Shane coming our way. She looks… happy. She's smiling and laughing along with Shane. My heart leaps into my throat when Whisper starts laughing. She pulls her head back to glance up at me and I peer down at the same time, raising an eyebrow in question.

"What?"

"Your heart is racing when you see her," she says softly, her eyes filled with love. Whisper is a hard girl to care about but my brother loves her and if I'm being honest, I love her too. Just not in the same way.

"No, you're just close to my cock," I tease. She laughs and slaps at me before pulling back and grabbing Shane's hand in hers. I watch as she drags her off toward the others. Liz stands there unsure of what to do with herself when I grab her hand and tug her into my body.

"You can touch me whenever you want." She laughs and looks up at me, her blond hair hanging around her shoulders.

"I didn't think I needed permission," she says.

"You don't. You just looked a little lost right then."

"Maybe I am." She shrugs.

"Why?"

"I don't know, Knox. I just feel like everything is spinning around me and I can't stop it. I don't know how to stop it."

"He won't hurt you," I remind her. I know that weighs heavily on her mind and I can't help that, but I can promise to protect her. And I will protect her.

"There's more than just me now that I'm worried about."

"Danny?" I ask. She shakes her head and turns to peer over her shoulder at everyone. Fuck. She cares about them as much as I do.

"Look at me," I tell her. She shakes her head and looks down. I grab her chin roughly in my hand and force her eyes to mine. "Do you really think that I'd put them in danger?"

"For me? Yes, I do." The growl that leaves my throat causes the people next to us to jump and walk away in a hurry. Shoving Liz's face away from me, I step back and take a deep breath. What the hell does she want from me?

"Then you clearly don't know me at all." I storm off, heading toward the guys and leaving her to fend for herself. I don't know why she feels the need to push me the way she does, and I don't know why I fucking like it so much. I'd never risk my family for anyone, but what Liz isn't realizing is that she's my goddamn family now too. I don't know what else to do to make her see that.

"I found one, Uncle Knox!" Bella yells and rushes toward me. She wraps her arms around my legs and the world around us could explode and I wouldn't give a shit. This, this little girl is what family should be like. Not the hell we lived.

"That is the best tree out here and you know what?"

"What?"

"While you were eating cookies and drinking hot chocolate, I got you all kinds of decorations for it," I tell her with a smile.

"You did?" Her little eyes light up.

"I did, but you have to do what Mommy and Daddy tell you when you get home first. I think nap time is coming," I tell her.

"I hate naps. I'm not a baby," she protests. I laugh.

"No but you still need a nap. I might need one too."

"Will you take a nap with me?" she asks hopefully.

"When I get back, I will." She hugs me once more before turning and skipping off to her mom.

"You make me sick," Steele says.

"Don't be jealous that she likes me better, man."

"Just because you act like a child," he muses.

"Jealousy isn't a good look on you." I aggravate him.

"My fist is going to be a good look on you though." We both laugh before I nod and look to Liz.

"I need to go. Jeremy should be on his way."

"You sure you don't want us there?" Steele asks. I shake my head.

"No. This is more important. Bella needs this. Besides, we have guys set up all around. He isn't that stupid," I remind him.

At least I hope he isn't. Steele nods and pulls me into a hug before turning and heading back to the tree. I turn to find Liz staring at me so intently that it makes me wonder what's running through that head of hers. Strolling toward her, I reach around and pull her hoodie up over her head, tucking her hair in while she keeps her eyes on me.

"What if he snaps?" she asks softly.

"What if I snap?" I ask in return as I finish tucking her hair back.

"I mean it, Knox."

"Me too, Liz. I don't know what else you need from me. I know I'm not the perfect man. I know I fuck things up basically on a daily basis, but I don't know what else I can give you. You have taken everything, every single part of me is resting in your hands." Her eyes fill with tears which isn't what I was going for this time. I just need her to understand that I don't have anything else to offer her. She has taken it all.

"I want you to have my heart."

"What?"

"I want you to have my heart, Knox."

"Then give it to me, Liz."

24

LIZ

I fidget with my hands as we sit in the booth waiting on Jeremy. Knox keeps checking his phone and to be honest, that's making me nervous. My knee bounces under the table and before I can think, his hand clamps around it. I glance over and see the look in his eyes. It's ready for a war. I'm not so sure that I am.

"Stop," he warns me.

"I'm trying."

"He isn't touching you," he growls. I know he won't. I know Knox won't let him hurt me but that isn't the point. Jeremy killed our mother for money. He's chased me across the country to get what he wants from me and now I'm about to come face-to-face with him. When I first met Knox, I thought he was a monster but nothing compares to Jeremy. I hear the jingle of the bell over the door as someone comes inside. I know it's him. There's a bad energy running through the room as Knox keeps his hand tightly wrapped around my knee. Each flex of his fingers has me sucking in another breath.

"I wasn't aware that this was a group discussion," Jeremy says, his voice slipping over me like ice. He drops into the seat across from us as I keep my head down.

"I wasn't aware I needed your goddamn permission to bring someone with me," Knox says, his tone low and full of hatred. Jeremy chuckles as I slowly raise my head to look at him. His eyes meet mine and the air is sucked from my lungs.

"You brought her along," he says, a smirk curling his lips.

"There's been a change in plans."

"What kind of change? Decided you didn't want her after all?" Jeremy asks, his voice dripping with controlled rage.

"No. I'm keeping her, that much you can be sure of." Knox's fingers flex on my knee almost to the point of pain. I swallow hard as Jeremy shifts in his seat.

"Spit it out, Knox. What the hell is she doing here? Signing the papers?"

"You bring them?" Knox asks. Jeremy smiles and pulls some paperwork out of his jacket pocket, setting it on the table in front of us. Knox's hand leaves my knee and moves to pick up the papers. He flips through them before pulling a pen from his own pocket. My heart beats rapidly in my chest as I wait to see what's about to happen.

"Sign it," Knox says, holding the pen out to me. I raise my shaky hand and reach for the pen as I stare down at the paper. When I don't move, Knox snaps. "I said sign it!" he roars. I jolt and bring the pen to the paper, signing my name quickly. Jeremy laughs across the table as he reaches up and slides the papers back toward him.

"Wasn't that easy? This could have ended a long time ago, Liz." Slowly, I drag my gaze to meet his and appraise him. The evil that I see in him now is a stark contrast to what I used to see. The more I learned about what he had done and why, I realized that evil was in there the whole time. I just wasn't privy to see it at the time. I was a pawn in his sick game. He was going to use me to his advantage and that almost worked. I raise my arms and rest my elbows on the table in front of me as I lean forward.

"You make me sick. You used me. You used her. She was all I had left and you took that away from me," I say through a soft sob.

"She was a drug addict."

"That you forced onto her. That wasn't her, she wasn't like that before."

"What difference does it make now? She's dead," he says with a chuckle. I nearly leap over the table, grabbing the front of his shirt on my way to his neck. He doesn't really respond but Knox does. He grabs me and jerks me back into my spot next to him.

"Enough!" he roars loudly.

"Get your toy under control, Knox." Jeremy adjusts his shirt then he folds the papers and slides them back into his pocket. Then it's Knox's turn. He leans forward, mimicking the way I was sitting with his arms on the table.

"My toy? No, she's more than that, Jeremy. I'm only going to say this once and hope to God that you get what I'm saying. She. Is. Mine. You come anywhere near her after this and I will kill you. I will take joy in ripping your beating heart out." Jeremy chuckles but I can tell by the tone in Knox's voice that he isn't joking around.

"Are you threatening me over her?" Jeremy leans in just like Knox is.

"Threatening? I don't threaten anyone and I think you are very well aware of that. If you so much as look her direction after today, I will kill you." Jeremy leans back in his seat and glances between the two of us as if he's bored and can't figure something out.

"What made you give a shit about her?"

"Everything. Liz, let's go," he says, ushering me out of my seat. I climb up quickly and he moves behind me. It's only seconds when Jeremy speaks again.

"Maybe I changed my mind." Knox's hands clench at his sides and whatever is about to happen isn't going to end well. He turns slowly to face Jeremy as he stands from his seat now as well.

"About?"

"Her. Maybe it isn't in my best interests to let her live." His words fuel the fear inside of me. I've run too much, have run too far for this to be it. He can't do this. I slowly peer up at Knox to see his nostrils flaring, his eyes narrowed. The muscles in his neck are corded tightly, his jaw tics.

"You want to know what's in your best interests? To walk out that door and never let me see your face around here again." His words hold power and authority but judging by the look on Jeremy's face, he doesn't give a shit.

"I'll let you play house for now, but that doesn't mean this is over," Jeremy adds. Knox steps toward him but I grab his hand in mine and tug him back.

"He's not worth it," I remind him. Knox isn't hearing it though. He's pissed.

"I warned you once. I won't tell you again after this. Come near her and you die. There is no other way around that." With that, Knox turns and drops my hand, pressing his to my back as he leads me out of the restaurant. He glances around, nodding at the men that linger nearby before ushering me into the truck. I climb in quickly and buckle as soon as I'm in. Knox walks around, keeping his eyes on the restaurant before he climbs in and slams the door. In seconds, his fists are balled up and he slams them into the steering wheel as he roars.

"This is bullshit!"

"I'm not scared of him, Knox."

"Fuck!"

"Knox?" I reach over and rest my hand on his arm, feeling his heat spiral through me. He slowly turns his head to glare at me, and I've never in my life seen this kind of anger in another person.

"You're mine, Liz."

"I know that, but if he comes after me, I will not put your family in danger," I remind him. I won't do it to them. They all mean too much to me at this point.

"That isn't your choice." His eyes are lost, feral.

"It is my choice," I remind him. His eyes narrow, nostrils flaring further as he leans across the seat. Each breath he takes is heavier than the last.

"You have no choices now, Liz. I call the goddamn shots. Don't. Test. Me."

25

KNOX

It's Christmas Eve. A day that we should all be celebrating and smiling. Except I'm not. I sit in the chair, my legs spread wide with a bottle of whiskey in my hand. Everything is weighing on me. Jeremy. The fact that Liz thinks she has a say in how this all goes down. It makes me sick to think about him going anywhere near her.

"Are you going to be an ass all night?" Whisper asks, dropping onto my knee.

"I'm not."

"You are. You're sulking and acting like a baby and honestly, it's pretty damn annoying," she says. I raise my head and peer up at her, wondering if she's joking with me right now. She's not. There is no smile on her face.

"Acting like a baby? Really? Care to explain that?" She shakes her head, pushing her hair over her shoulder.

"Poor little Knox didn't get his own way. What's wrong? You can't force her to do what you want? You guys didn't seem to have a problem fighting me so why aren't you fighting her?" she asks, eyebrows raised.

"You think I'm not fighting her?" She shakes her head. "She knows the deal, Whisper. I fucking dare her to step out of line on this." Acid eats at my insides as I think about her going against what I say. The meeting with Jeremy was only a week ago but it feels like forever. It feels like I should be out there hunting this little bastard.

"You dare me?" Pulling my gaze to meet Liz's, I smirk.

"You heard that right. This is my show now, Liz. You have no say in how this goes down," I remind her smoothly.

"Is that what you think? I never asked you to take over for me, Knox. I can handle this on my own." Now, I shove Whisper off my lap and stand from my chair. Taking a long pull from the whiskey bottle, I set it on the table and stalk toward her.

"By running?" I ask, cocking my head to the side as I wait for her answer.

"We were supposed to be having a good time tonight," Steele growls as he comes into the room.

"We're having a great time, aren't we Liz?" She narrows her eyes at me and I can't help but smile. This girl pushes my goddamn buttons and I think I like it a little more than I should.

"Then why is she pissed?" Steele asks, stepping up next to her. His arm comes out, wrapping around her shoulders and pulling her closer. A growl lodges in my throat. I don't care that he's my brother, I don't want him touching her anymore. That was a one and done.

"She isn't."

"Like hell I'm not! You don't run my life, Knox." Now I step into her space, closing the distance between us.

"If I say you stay back, it's for your own good, Liz." My tone has softened but that lump in my chest is still there. She makes it hard to breathe, hard to think.

"He's not wrong," Steele says, backing away from her.

"Do I look like some kind of baby to you two?" she squeals and looks between us.

"Not at all, but you also don't realize what you're up against. Your brother shot and killed your mom while you watched, Liz. What the hell do you think he'll do to you?" I watch the fire in her eyes slowly fade as reality hits her. She knows what he can do. She saw it.

"I don't like the idea of being around here when the time comes," she admits and I understand. Grabbing her face in my hands, I force her to look at me, in the eye.

"I get it. I do, but guess what? The ones that are going to protect you are all in this room, Liz. The ones that will have your back are standing behind you right now. Me. I'm right here in front of you, Liz." Her tongue sweeps out over her lips as I watch her, waiting for an answer. I want to see anything, something that resembles understanding in her. So when she slowly begins nodding her head, I smile.

"Okay, but—"

"No. No buts. Just okay. We're going to go out to Intensity tonight, then tomorrow we are going to watch Bella have an amazing Christmas. After that, we'll talk about the other shit with Jeremy. I think this family needs a little normalcy for a short time," I tell her. She nods her head and I lean down and capture her lips with mine. Each brush of our lips sends a sizzle down my spine. Each time I touch this girl, my brain fogs up.

"Mommy?" I pull away when I hear Bella come into the room. We all turn to look at her.

"Yeah?"

"Is Santa coming?" God, I didn't know having a niece could make me feel so much. I love that little girl.

"He is but you have to be a good girl and go to sleep," Shane tells her. Bella smiles and hugs her mom before making her way around the room. When she gets to me, I lift her into my arms as she hugs my neck.

"Uncle Knox?"

"Yeah, baby girl?"

"I think this is going to be the best Christmas ever!"

"Why is that?"

"I think Santa is going to bring me a puppy." I chuckle and press a kiss to her cheek before saying, "Is that what you told him?" She nods her head rapidly before wiggling to free herself of my hold. I set her on her feet once more and watch her take off for the stairs. The babysitter is already here and up there waiting for her.

"We ready?" Steele asks. Whisper heads for the door and we all follow.

"What did she say?"

"She said Santa is bringing her a puppy," I tell Liz. Her mouth falls open, and she glances around quickly before pulling her gaze back to mine.

"I don't think they are getting her a puppy," she says.

"Maybe not but I know a guy," I say with a wink.

"You aren't going to ask them?"

"No. I don't need permission to buy my niece a puppy," I say. Liz giggles and it's the best thing I've heard in days. Everyone piles into Steele's truck, but I opt to take my own so that when we're done, I can make a pit stop. Holding the door for Liz, she climbs in shaking her head.

"What?" I ask.

"You are the best uncle to that little girl."

"She's a good kid."

"It's not just that."

"Then what is it?" I ask, leaning closer to her a little more.

"It's you. You're amazing."

26

LIZ

The music is perfect, the lighting dancing over the floor in Christmas green and red. There are decorations dangling from the ceiling. Everything is perfect. So why am I so worried? I know Jeremy is out there somewhere, it's almost as if I can feel it. I can sense him somewhere.

"Stop overthinking and dance with me," Knox hollers over the music. I smile up at him and wrap my arms around his neck. Ed Sheeran's remix of *Shape of You* blasts through the speakers as Knox starts moving. The beat thumps in my chest as we dance. Everyone is having an amazing time. I see Steele and Whisper out of the corner of my eye, she's laughing, her head thrown back. Shane and Callan are pulled in closely to each other. It makes me happy to see them all like this.

"Come on, Liz," Knox whispers in my ear before biting the lobe. I moan as he pushes his body closer to mine. His hips move, rolling to the beat of the music as he keeps me close. Grabbing my hand, he spins me out before pulling me back into his hard chest before doing it again. I laugh this time as he smiles at me. My hips sway on their own, his hands landing directly on them. Sweat trickles down my temples as the heat in the room kicks up a notch. The louder the music goes; the closer Knox gets. It's amazing to see the way this man moves, and it's even better feeling his muscles shift and move under my palms. I'm lost in his gaze when Leddy comes over the speaker.

"We're going to slow it down for the couples now! It is Christmas after all. Just this once!" I laugh as Berlin's *Take My Breath Away* comes over the speakers. Knox chuckles and pulls me into his body as he moves us around the floor. Even with a slow song, his moves make it sexy as hell. His hands stay around me, keeping me within his warm embrace. I rest my head on his chest listening to the rapid beating of his heart. I know that heart. It's a heart that doesn't stop when it wants something. It's a heart that cares and loves. It's a heart that I want to hold onto forever.

The night goes on with more dancing and fun. I don't think I've ever had a Christmas Eve like this one. Knox leans down and kisses my neck before moving to my ear.

"You ready to go?"

"Where?" I ask over the music. He winks at me and I know what he's doing. I smirk and shake my head before grabbing his hand in mine. He laughs as he leads me toward the door, stopping to tell the guys that we were leaving. Once we get outside everything changes. The man that was taking his time and dancing with me now has me pinned against the wall outside. The music still blasts through the walls but it's him that I feel. His lips are on mine, kissing me like he's a man starved. His hand knots in my hair, keeping my head where he wants me and I let him. I don't care. I just want to feel all that Knox has to give. His soft lips dance with mine and everything is perfect. We're both breathing heavily when he pulls back, resting his forehead against mine.

"You're perfect. You know that right?" His words seep into my heart making it beat a little faster.

"Not even close," I laugh.

"For me you are. Don't ever change who you are, Liz." My mouth opens and closes but what do I say to that? How do I respond? This man has given me everything that I never knew I needed. He's made me feel things that I've kept locked away for a long time. Everything I wanted to keep hidden, Knox has torn out of me.

"I could say the same to you," I whisper. He chuckles and presses his lips to mine one more time before grabbing my hand and pulling me toward the truck.

"You like when I'm an asshole?" he asks, smiling over his shoulder at me.

"You are perfect, Knox. Even when you're an asshole. You always seem to know what I need and when I need it," I admit to him. That's not something that I wanted to tell him or like to admit but it's true.

"I don't plan on stopping that anytime soon."

"I don't know that I'd like you if you did." He opens the door and ushers me into the truck, slapping my ass on the way in. I laugh and get settled into my seat as I watch him walk around the front. When he gets in, his scent wraps around me.

"Ready to go get a puppy?"

"Cal is going to kill you; you know that right?" Knox starts the truck and pulls out of the parking lot. He texted his friend earlier and told him what he needed and he agreed to meet him. A chill runs slowly down my spine as I gaze out the window. I don't know what it is but I can feel it. I rub my arms trying to warm the cold that now seeps into my bones.

"You okay?"

"I don't know. I just feel a little weird," I tell him. Knox reaches over and places his hand on my leg, giving it a squeeze of reassurance. The drive doesn't take long and when he pulls off at a small park, I glance around once more. It's empty. It is Christmas Eve after all, but that does little to ease the feeling that slowly sinks in deeper.

"Let's get out. He'll be here soon," Knox says. I watch him climb out and come around the truck. He opens my door and I hop out as he grabs my hand.

"It's dark."

"You scared of the dark now?" he teases. This playful side of Knox is sweet but I don't know how to take him. He's always bossy and demanding but this? It's… nice.

"No. It just feels odd."

"It should." And there it is. The voice that could cause my blood to run cold. Knox drops my hand and spins around to come face-to-face with Jeremy and Tommy. There's a sick smile on Jeremy's face that causes vomit to burn the back of my throat.

"What the fuck are you doing here?" Knox asks, crossing his arms over his chest.

"I told you I changed my mind," Jeremy says casually with the shrug of his shoulders.

"And I told you to stay out of my way," Knox hisses. Jeremy chuckles before snapping his fingers. Two more men move out of the shadows as I gasp. Knox moves to step in front of me when all hell breaks loose. Jeremy lunges, Tommy moves in, and the other guys rush toward us. In a whirlwind of punches, screams, growls and roars, I'm knocked to the ground. My head spins when it collides with the concrete. A dog growling can be heard but as I blink my eyes, it's hard to see.

"You son of a bitch!" I hear Knox roar as I shove myself up. Someone kneels next to me, grabbing my arm and ripping me from the ground. Gun shots ring through the night sky causing me to scream. Flashbacks of that night flash behind my eyes.

He's standing there, the gun raised and aimed at her. I'm shaking, slowly falling down the dark hole that my own brother created.

"Liz!" I hear Knox before I hear a huff. Shaking my head, I try to get my bearings when some pulls me again.

"Get off me," I scream, wiggling and trying to fight.

"Calm down, I'm Knox's friend." I slowly calm as I blink my eyes and focus. There's a dog hanging off Jeremy's arm, a man standing over Tommy and the other two guys that were with them on the ground unmoving. I gasp when I take it all in, tears spilling down my cheeks. Knox stumbles and moves toward me, pulling me into his arms. I wrap my arms around him only to feel the warmth under my fingertips.

"Oh my God," I whisper.

"It's okay, Liz. I'm okay."

"What do you want to do with that one?" the man that was holding me asks. Knox keeps me tucked against him as he turns us slightly.

"Get rid of him," he growls. I see the man nod as he walks away from us and calls off his dog. The dog instantly moves away from Jeremy and stands by his owner's side. My heart is beating rapidly in my chest as I take in the gruesome scene.

"Liz? Are you okay?" Knox's voice is soft, too soft. I nod my head and bury my face back in the front of his chest. I hear Jeremy yelling something before the silence takes over. My body trembles as I'm lifted and carried back to the truck. Knox puts me in and closes the door. When I lift my head, I see him talking to the guy with the dog. I jump when someone knocks on the window on the driver's side. When I glance over, a woman pulls the door open and shoves a big black puppy inside.

"This is what Knox paid for. I'm not sure what happened out there," she says happily as if there aren't dead bodies laying a few feet away. Siren's sound in the distance but no one seems concerned about it. This is it. Jeremy is dead. It doesn't seem real but when I glance past the woman, I can see him unmoving on the ground. Then I look to the puppy as it stares at me. That dog, the big one attacked him.

"Boulder is a protection dog. He's been trained for it. Top of his class. This little guy can be trained too," the lady adds. Is this normal? Is she used to seeing dead bodies? Is that why she doesn't seem concerned. When I don't answer her, she closes the door and walks away. I don't know what to feel, what to think. This is insane.

A few minutes later, Knox climbs in the truck and drives off without saying a word.

27

———

KNOX

I roll over and grab her face in my hands, kissing her until she melts beneath me. She tastes like tears. My tears. She's giving them to me and I can't think of a better Christmas present than this. My cock is hard and pressing against her. She arches her back, pressing herself into me. I groan into her mouth before she slides her hand down my side. Reaching between us, she puts me where she wants me. I thrust into her, listening as she moans into my mouth. Last night was hell. She cried, she shook. She was so afraid, but the more we talked, the more she calmed. I told her that everything was taken care of and that no one would ever bother her again. She slowly came to understand and then cried herself to sleep in my arms. All I've wanted was for her to cry for me and she did just that. Except this time was different. This time she gave me all of her.

"Knox?" She says my name breathlessly.

"Hmm?"

"If I tell you something, will you promise not to freak out?" I thrust one long thrust inside of her, making her groan before I sit up and look down at her.

"Tell me what?"

"Promise you won't freak out?"

"I don't promise shit, Liz. What the hell is it?" I demand as my cock throbs inside of her. What is it with women and wanting to wait until a man is balls deep inside of her to talk? Fuck!

"I love you." My heart stops in my chest as I lower my gaze to her. Her hair is splayed out on the pillow, her bright puffy eyes staring up at me. I lean down, brushing my lips over hers. I listen to her groan as I move my hips.

"I know," I say softly. She sighs and raises her hips to meet mine. Each thrust is better than the last. Each touch of our bodies together just cements how much I needed this girl in my life. Rotating my hips, she moans louder and digs her nails into my back.

"Fuck, Liz!" Harder and faster, I take her. She's so fucking tight and made just for me. As my balls tighten and my cock jerks, I say, "I love you, Liz." Her nails dig deeper, pulling my body into hers. Her head comes up, her lips devouring mine like a crazed woman and I want it. I want it all.

We're both panting and out of breath when the dog starts whimpering.

"Are you sure that was the best kind of dog to get Bella?"

"Yeah, why?"

"Well, that one last night… What it did."

"He's trained for that. This thing isn't. They are good family dogs regardless of what people think. You can train any dog to be a protection dog. Look at him. He's harmless." I smile as I peer over the side of the bed. When I pull out of her, she crawls over and peeks over the edge at the giant black puppy.

"He is pretty cute," she says. He jumps up, putting his front feet on the side of the bed and I reach down and scratch his head.

"He is. You think she will like him?"

"Are you okay, Knox?"

"Don't change the subject, Liz. I'm fine. It was a flesh wound. Now, do you think she will like him?" I know she was worried all night about me, but I'm fine. A flesh wound is nothing I haven't dealt with before. She shifts and sits up on the bed as I do the same.

"She will love him, but I think Callan might kill you," she says with a smile. Her eyes roam over the bandage on my shoulder when I grab her chin in between my fingers.

"I'm fine. Look at me," I order her. She moves her gaze to mine and damn, I love looking at her. "I'm fine and it's all over, Liz. This is it. This is us."

"Us," she says softly.

"Yes, us. There's no more you or me. It's us." She nods her head and as I lean in about to press my lips to hers, there's a banging on the door.

"Uncle Knox! Santa was here!" The dog doesn't even bark.

"We're coming!" I call back. I peek over the side of the bed and roll my eyes. "So much for a watch dog."

"He didn't even bark," Liz giggles. I climb off the bed and grab my sweatpants, pulling them on. Tossing Liz her clothes, she stands and dresses too.

"You ready for this?" I ask.

"I can't wait to see her face," she says, reaching down to pick the dog up. With him in her arms, he licks her face causing her to laugh. I slip my hand into the drawer and grab the small box out and slide it into my pocket before she sees me.

"Let's get down there," I say, heading for the door. Liz follows behind me as we make our way down the steps. Bella is tearing through the presents we put out last night. Her smile is the brightest thing that I've ever seen. It does my heart good to see my family happy for a change. I don't think there is anything better than this.

"What the fuck is that?" Callan's voice thunders through the room.

"That is a Cane Corso," I inform him. He shakes his head, anger in his eyes.

"A puppy!" Bella rushes toward Liz as she leans down and hands off the puppy.

"You didn't," Callan hisses.

"Oh, I did. Told you I was the best uncle," I remind him.

"For fuck's sake. I'm not cleaning up the shit!" Steele grumbles. I grab Liz as Bella shows off her new dog to her parents. I'm not good at this stuff. Slipping my hand in my pocket, I pull the box out and hold it out to Liz. My stomach is in knots. I don't know if I'm making the right choice. I don't know if this is what I'm supposed to do with my life, but what I do know is that I'm never letting Liz out of my sight again.

"What's this?" she asks, peering up at me. I reach over with my free hand and pop the lid open. Her eyes follow before widening. The diamond sparkles in the early morning sunlight.

"Knox?"

"This is us, Liz. This is me and you," I tell her. She looks up at me and then back at the ring.

"Are you sure? You barely know me. I've been nothing but trouble," she rambles. I pull the ring from the box and grab her hand in mine. Sliding the ring on her finger feels like the right thing to do. My heart races just like every other time I'm near her.

"I know that I can't breathe when you're not near me. I know that you mean more to me than any other person ever has. I love you, Liz. I won't lose you again. Say you'll stay with me forever." She looks up with tears in her eyes before leaping into my arms. She presses her lips to mine and that's all the yes I need.

"Uncle Knox!" Bella yells. I reluctantly pull my lips from Liz to gaze at my niece.

"Do you like your puppy?" She nods excitedly.

"I love him! Did you get what you wanted from Santa?" Her bright eyes are so much like her mom's. She's perfect.

Turning my head to gaze down at Liz, I nod.

"I got more than I wanted."

The end.

AFTERWORD

That was it! I hope you enjoyed the Alder Academy Trilogy! Watch out for more bully romance in the future!

Connect with Erin and find more of her hot romance books!

Connect with Erin! She loves her stalkers.

Newsletter:http://bit.ly/ErinTrejoNewsletter

BookBub:

https://www.bookbub.com/authors/erin-trejo

Facebook:

https://www.facebook.com/authorerintrejo/

Facebook Readers Group –Fire and Ice https://www.facebook.com/groups/1177887305577544/

Amazon:

https://www.amazon.com/Erin-Trejo/e/B00U0RXH80/ Twitter: https://twitter.com/trejo_erin

IG:https://www.instagram.com/authorerintrejo/